PUFFIN BOO

Editor: Kaye W

RUTH CRA

'Feel them,' said the old man, and Ruth put her hand nervously into the hollow where the baby hedgehogs lay. It was a new experience to her, but then everything that had happened since they came to Llanwern on holiday was a new experience.

Her father had died in a road accident, and her mother and younger sister lay injured in hospital. She was still Ruth Crane, the clever American girl, but now they might be poor, they might even be going to live in Llanwern, the simple Welsh village where her mother had grown up, and Ruth felt that a little knowledge of cooking and cleaning would have been far more useful than all her brains and booklearning.

She also had her young brother Tony to cope with. She'd never bothered much with Tony before, but now they were on their own together at their aunt's house, Ruth was beginning to see some sense in him at last, and in her cousin Pete, whom she'd last seen years before when they were both eleven. People were interesting, she thought, and cookery too, and she was going to learn plenty about both.

This is Alison Morgan's third book to be published in Puffins and, although it may easily be read on its own, many familiar characters from the previous books appear in it. The first, *Fish*, has been serialized on television, and *Pete*, the second, was awarded a Welsh Arts Council Literature Prize for 1973.

For readers of eleven and over.

Alison Morgan

RUTH CRANE

PUFFIN BOOKS

Puffin Books, Penguin Books Ltd, Harmondsworth, Middlesex, England
Penguin Books Inc., 7110 Ambassador Road, Baltimore, Maryland 21207, U.S.A.
Penguin Books Australia Ltd, Ringwood, Victoria, Australia
Penguin Books Canada Ltd, 41 Steelcase Road West, Markham, Ontario, Canada
Penguin Books (N.Z.) Ltd, 182-190 Wairau Road, Auckland 10, New Zealand

—

First published by Chatto & Windus 1973
Published in Puffin Books 1976

—

Copyright © Alison Morgan, 1973

—

Made and printed in Great Britain
by Hazell Watson & Viney Ltd,
Aylesbury, Bucks
Set in Linotype Plantin

To Gillian

Chapter 1

'I WISH she was dead,' said Ruth.

Out of the corner of her eye she could see Pete keeping his face carefully still, trying to look as though he were too absorbed in his book to have heard her.

He's pretending, she thought, because he doesn't know what to say. But in her heart she knew she was pretending, too. Not about wishing Patsy were dead, but in saying it, saying it aloud so that Pete should hear, and in the kind of voice that she hoped would make him think she was speaking her thoughts aloud by mistake.

As soon as she had said the words, she could hear them hang self-consciously in the air. 'I wish she was dead.' It was what she had been thinking, and yet all the time there was this second strand running through her mind, wanting other people to know her secret thoughts, to know how unhappy she was, and yet not wanting them to know that she wanted them to know.

Pete elaborately turned a page, and the silence hung between them as his eye followed the meaningless print.

'Why?' he said at last, braced to play his part, but the pause had been too long and Ruth lost her nerve.

'Why what?' she said.

'Why what you said?'

'What did I say? I didn't think I had said anything.'

Pete looked at her, expressionless. 'Sorry. My mistake.'

Ruth got up. 'I'd better go look for Tony,' she said, and walked out of the room.

She did not go straightaway. She knew Tony was playing with some other small boys up at Thomas's farm on the outskirts of the village, and from the garden behind the house she could hear their voices drifting over the fields. She could pick out Tony's from the others because it was higher and shriller, and because she knew it so well she fancied she could detect the American accent. Tony had lived in New York all his life, but before he was born Ruth and Patsy had been brought up in England, until their Welsh mother and American father had moved to the United States.

Tony is happy, she thought, and envy stabbed her aloof sorrow. Tony was happy running around with his friends, and as soon as he felt unhappy he would come wailing around Auntie Mary, Pete's mother, who would cosset him. He had always had everything the easy way, even his troubles, and never more so than now, when it was she, Ruth, who was expected to be the one to comfort him, the strong elder sister at this moment in their family crisis.

She stood by the gate leading into the field behind the house, scratching the lichen from the gate-post, and tried to look straight and hard at the new pattern of her life.

For a dreamlike fortnight, this isolated village in Wales had been the setting for a story-book holiday in which the successful American lecturer brought his family to revisit the scenes of his wife's childhood. From the metallic world of skyscrapers and cars and air terminals they had dropped like pebbles into a yielding land of earth and leaf, where green and brown and blue were not alternative colours you could choose from the decorator's shade card, but the notes of a tune played by the light upon the changing seasons of growth and death. This year's green blade was next year's brown earth and the grey Welsh rain mocked the distinction between blue sky, green tree, brown earth.

Here the Cranes fell soundlessly into a community that asked politely about their successful way of life in New York, but had

8

to excuse itself to milk the cows before the answering was half-done, yet could lean on the garden gate for hours reminiscing with Mum about schooldays half a generation ago in the village school that still stood behind its white railings across the stream.

Ruth had enjoyed it. Patsy and Tony, although they threw themselves happily into the local children's activities, were inclined to show off, hoping to amaze the natives with a display of sophistication, but Ruth felt herself a traveller wrapped in a cloak of invisibility. She had no wish to be noticed or admired; that would come later, when she got back to New York and would write penetrating essays for her teachers about the Welsh way of life, and amuse her contemporaries with portraits of the local characters.

But now it was all different; there would be no going back. It was like going to sleep one night and having a dream and waking in the morning to find that the dream had become the reality and everything one had accepted as real had turned into yesterday's dream.

It had all happened so quickly. They were driving back to London Airport in the car that their father had hired for the fortnight's holiday. They had just passed through the toll-gates on the English side of the Severn bridge, and already the Welsh dream was fading, when a lorry in front had swerved uncontrollably across their path and as they slewed sickeningly towards the great hulk in front of them Ruth could hear the crescendo of screaming brakes on the vehicle behind.

The screaming had been the last thing she had heard before the impact, and the first thing she was conscious of afterwards. For a moment she had felt it was still all to happen, but then she realized it was a different sound − that of a child screaming. She opened her eyes to find Tony sitting bolt upright beside her, open-mouthed, yelling and shaking her. There were people all round the car, pulling at the crumpled doors, shouting at each other, sounds of sirens, grinding traffic, slamming

9

doors, but inside the car all was still except for the noise Tony was making.

Ruth drew her mind sharply away from probing the next few hours. There had been noise, and fear, and endless waiting among strangers, and over all a sense of complete unreality that had persisted until the present moment.

With her mind, she knew very well what had happened. Her father was dead, her mother in Bristol hospital, and Patsy – bouncing, loyal, comical Patsy – was lying in a coma in another hospital in Newport. It was only when she thought of Patsy that the web of unreality that enmeshed her tore a little and let in a rush of icy air.

Her father's death was oddly the easiest thing to accept. He had always been a remote, elderly-seeming person who did not concern himself much with his children's affairs except when he was seized with one of his enthusiasms for a system of life. Then he would suddenly descend upon the household routines and impose a new arbitrary pattern upon them until he wearied of putting theories into practice in such infertile ground and returned to the less intractable areas of academic discussion.

'It wouldn't be so bad,' Ruth once complained bitterly to her mother, 'if it ever once occurred to him that we do have our own way of living when he isn't busy organizing us.' She remembered sullenly being put through the hoops of some patent method of learning to read long after she had in fact mastered the art of reading by normal traditional methods, simply because her father never thought to discover what his children were doing before deciding they would be better doing something else. There had been scenes about six months ago when he had decided the whole family needed to follow a course of fitness exercises that were designed to benefit inactive university lecturers but which Patsy furiously claimed lost her a place in her school junior basketball team because he insisted on her doing exercises for the good of her health at a time when she should have been at extra games practice.

Ruth sighed. One should grieve for one's father when he is dead, of course, and she supposed as time passed she would miss him, but at the moment – she had to admit it guiltily – the sense of loss was more than outweighed by the romantic aura that surrounded an orphan. If it had been her mother, now ... the sense of relief that it was not her mother was the one concrete source of joy she could hold on to in these strange twilight days. Her mother was seriously ill, she knew, but she was now off the danger list and it was only a matter of time till she could be moved, first to a hospital nearer Llanwern, where Ruth could visit her more often, and later to start the unknown family life that awaited them.

Ruth's uncle and aunt had taken her to see her mother in hospital, and it had been unexpectedly reassuring; so many people had told her kindly not to be alarmed at her mother's weakness, or the hospital's paraphernalia of tubes and bottles and machines that surrounded her, that it was unbelievably comforting to see her smiling in her usual placid way, and speaking naturally about arrangements for the children in that soft Welsh accent that the years in New York had never eradicated.

It was only when her mother spoke of Patsy that the serenity quivered, and Ruth resolved that whatever other people might say she must go and see Patsy.

Even her mother told her not to, not yet. 'She's not conscious,' she said. 'As soon as she comes round and asks for one of us, if I'm not well enough to go, then you must go. But until she does ...' that was where she paused to take a breath '... then you're best looking after Tony. He needs you, you know he does.'

He doesn't, you know, Ruth had thought, even then, but Mom was soft about Tony, always had been, and though it had made him thoroughly objectionable, now wasn't the time to say so.

'Don't worry,' she said. 'I expect Patsy will be coming to see *you* before very long.'

Auntie Mary had broken in then, talking rather too fast and brightly, and that was when Ruth first realized just how ill Patsy might be. Only concussion, probably, they had said, whereas Mom had broken ribs and punctured lungs and a score of other injuries, and was chatting away in bed making plans and smiling pleasantly.

Afterwards, driving back over the same fateful Severn bridge, she had insisted that she must go and see Patsy in Newport. Auntie Mary tried to dissuade her, but Mr Jenkins, a man of long silences, said quietly, 'It's her right,' and instead of turning into the winding roads leading up into the heart of Wales, followed the motorway along to Newport at the same steady forty miles an hour that was all his ancient little saloon could do.

Ruth found she had gathered a handful of rough dry fragments of lichen from the top of the gate. She stared at it unseeing for a moment, then threw it impatiently away and went through into the field. She began to walk slowly across it in the direction of Thomas's farm. She did not particularly want to see Tony, and there was no need to fetch him home yet, but it was something to do.

She had never had much use for Tony. His babyish and demanding ways had irritated her even when he was still of an age when most adults thought he was cute; now that he was nine she noticed the charm beginning to wear thin even on adults. It had embarrassed Ruth on this holiday; here in this quiet village in Wales nine-year-old boys were responsible members of the community, helping on the farm or taking themselves off on expeditions on their bicycles, whereas Tony expected to be waited on at every turn. Ruth wished he would have the grace to try and hide his helplessness and at least pretend to be more grown-up than he was, but that was not in his nature.

Before the disaster she had watched, uncomfortably, Auntie Mary and the other Welsh relatives grow a little frosty towards Tony, but now they all exuded unlimited love and forbearance, and he revelled in it. Far from needing Ruth, he was mothered by every woman in the village. Boys constantly turned up at the cottage, dispatched by their mothers, to ask him to play, and when anything crossed him he had only to cry for Auntie Mary and he was taken home by kindly elder sisters or given a ride back on the farm tractor. His aunt, looking worn and pre-occupied, tried to cook his favourite foods and patiently found jobs for him around her in the kitchen and uncomplainingly did them herself when he left them scarcely started. The only gap in caring for Tony that was left for Ruth to fill was the task of putting him in his place.

'Shut up, Tony,' she would say at last, goaded out of her melancholy, or 'Don't be such a baby'; then he would whimper to Auntie Mary that he wanted Mommy, and be comforted.

'What about me?' Ruth wanted to cry, but she could not.

Not that Auntie Mary was ever anything but kind and understanding to her, too, but Ruth's reserve stood deep and uncrossable between them.

She knew the strain was telling on Auntie Mary, because she jumped on poor Pete with ten times the ferocity that Ruth dared show to Tony – but then Pete was her own son, and four-teen, and was living in his own village with his father and mother and Uncle Sam, the local policeman, all around him, and his grandparents a mile up the road, and a whole host of other relations in the next village, so his mother could nag him as much as she liked and nobody need feel sorry for him.

Ruth did, though, a little. He had come home from spending a fortnight with his father at his place of work up in Scot-land on the day when he had expected his American cousins to be leaving, and walked straight into the disaster. He had been

13

pushed out of his own room and sent to sleep with Uncle Sam over the road, and during the turmoil of collecting Ruth and Tony, visiting their mother and Patsy, arranging for their father's funeral, the one person whose comfort nobody seemed to concern themselves with was Pete. 'He'll manage,' his mother would say, her mind on other things. He did, of course; getting his own supper, waiting in for the coal man, fetching extra bread, cadging dinner off the Thomases, making up the fire – and in between making himself useful being utterly forgotten.

Poor dazed Pete. He had hardly spoken a word since he got back, and the last time Ruth had met him was over two years ago when they were both eleven, and he had seemed shy and uninterested. I wish I had told him about Patsy, she thought suddenly. He was the nearest thing to Patsy around, and Patsy was the only person Ruth had ever been able to talk to properly.

What had seemed so terrible about visiting Patsy was that at first Ruth had thought the cubicle where they took her was empty – empty, that is, apart from various bits of furniture like the bed and the locker and the trolley and the bedclothes piled on the bed. It was the way the nurses behaved that made her think the room was empty, concentrating on Ruth and Auntie Mary as though there was nothing else that deserved their attention; not like visiting her mother when everyone made sure first that she was ready for them, and put on their bright hospital voices when approaching her bed.

And then Ruth had suddenly realized that the pile of bed-clothes was Patsy – Patsy so deeply unconscious that for the nurses, who had never seen her in any other state, she simply did not exist as a person at all.

They had not stayed long; there was nothing to stay for. Even Auntie Mary was visibly daunted and white as she made silly inconsequential remarks about telling Patsy they had called as soon as she came round, and the hospital was to let her know immediately she started asking for them. Ruth had not spoken about Patsy then or since – apart from just now to Pete, when she had tried to, and failed.

It was funny how well she and Patsy had always got on together. In theory they had every reason to dislike each other; Ruth, set apart for as long as she could remember by being 'the clever one', the one that teachers never asked to answer questions in the ordinary hit-and-miss routine of class, but only when everyone else had failed, might so easily have been scornful and resentful of Patsy's gift for instant friendship with everyone she met; and Patsy could easily have tried to underline her own popularity as being a far more valuable asset than the lonely peaks of academic excellence. But it had never worked out like that. Being clever was something Ruth had grown to accept in the same way that a polio victim accepts a wheel-chair – a convenient means of dealing with life but something that set her apart from almost everybody else.

Not Patsy, though. Ruth's uncanny ability to know the answers was something that just did not interest Patsy; she liked to be with Ruth simply because she was Ruth.

In return, Ruth, who would think up a dozen replies and have to select one of them to fit the occasion when she was with anyone else, said whatever came into her mind to Patsy. She was mildly proud of the fact that Patsy always had lots of friends just as Patsy was mildly proud of having a sister who was always top of the class, but it didn't actually have much connection with the way they felt about each other.

And now Patsy was lying unconscious in hospital among strangers, incapable of making friends with any of them. She might die like that quite soon, or live like that for years and years.

'But she probably won't,' said Ruth, trying to convince herself. 'She'll probably get quite okay again, quite soon; that's what everybody tells me, so why shouldn't I believe them?' She wished she could, but after that moment on the motorway she felt she would never again live with the feeling that misfortunes were things that happened to other people.

She had been trailing rather aimlessly across the meadow, following the well-worn track beaten by Pete and his friend Tom at the farm, without looking up to see where she was going. Now she straightened herself deliberately as though to throw off her anxiety, and glanced ahead. In front a gate opened on to a lane immediately opposite the entrance to Tygwyn farm, and a short steep track ran up to the buildings grouped around a broad concreted yard.

To Ruth's surprise, a man was leaning on the gate, with his back to her, gazing intently up towards the farm. He was nobody she knew, a shabby man with one arm resting on a shotgun laid along the top of the gate, and a dead rabbit hanging from the other hand. His figure, small and wiry in the old-fashioned tweed jacket and corduroy trousers, looked youthful, but the hair that straggled over his collar was grey.

Ruth paused uncertainly, because the man seemed quite unaware of her approach and she did not know how to draw attention to herself. However, to her surprise, he shifted over without looking round and motioned as though to invite her to come and share his view.

'It's a great game they're having, whatever,' he remarked companionably, and continued to stare up the farm track.

The boys had laid out an assault course of hay-bales in the steep lane and were negotiating it with a home-made go-cart. There were four of them; Tony, and Gary Thomas from the farm, who were just finishing the course, and two of Gary's friends, Fish and Jimmy Price, who as soon as the other two came to a halt seized the go-cart and hauled it back up to have their turn.

'It's races they're having, see,' said the man. 'Two of them lads has got watches, and they're timing it, see.' He paused a minute, resettling his cap on his head as he thought it out. 'Course, if they don't finish without they runs into one of them bales, then it counts against them. That's what I reckon.' He

16

turned an innocent earnest face to Ruth, and between the grey wispy hair and the grey stubble his eyes were bright and joyful. 'It don't count so much if they make mistakes. That's fair, that is. That boy with the light hair, that your brother?'

'Yes,' said Ruth, surprised.

'Thought as much,' said the man. 'Strangers?'

'Do you live round here, then?' asked Ruth. If so, it was strange she had never seen him. She had a feeling he was the kind of person she ought to be scared of, but he wasn't scary, not in the least.

'Ssh!' said the man. 'They're off!' His whole concentration was fixed on the battered old go-cart skidding and lurching between the bales. His mouth and eyebrows reflected every crisis in the helter-skelter descent and his fingers gripped the gun as though he were pulling on the guide-rope himself as they hurtled through one particularly tight corner. Only when the boys slowed down at the end did he let his breath out in a long sigh.

'Hell,' he said, 'that was the best run yet. The best yet.' He looked at Ruth, his face alight with enthusiasm; then disappointment dawned. 'Course, you didn't see the other runs? Pity.' He shook his head. 'Pity you didn't see the one before. Pity, that.'

'I expect they'll go again,' said Ruth, to console him.

'That one, your brother, him with the light hair, he isn't quite so daring. Not as bold as them others. He'll come, mind, give him time, he'll come,' he added, anxious in case he had offended her. 'They all come in the end, give 'em time. You can't rush 'em. No good ever come of rushing 'em.'

'Do you live round here?' Ruth tried again.

'I'll tell you what, if you rush 'em it don't do a bit of good. I wouldn't be surprised if it didn't make 'em slower, when you come to think about it. Oh, aye, I live hereabouts most of the time. Getting a bit old for the winters, though. They mostly knows me, hereabouts.'

17

'Where do you live then?'

'Wait, now, they'll be off in a minute. That Jimmy, there, he'll give the signal – he's the one with the watch, see. You watch, now, you'll see what I mean about the fair-headed lad, your ... hey, they're off! Going well now ... steady ... steady ... well done then ... it's a good run, a very good run, the best these boys have done ... he's getting the way of it, that lad, he's ... aah, damn!'

Disappointment slumped in every line of his body as the go-cart came spectacularly to grief halfway down the course. Predictably, it was Tony who burst into wails.

'Pity,' said the man. 'Just as they was going so well. They might have beaten the others, I reckon, the way they was going.' He stood back from the gate, as though expecting Ruth to open it and go through to her brother.

She supposed she ought to, and anyway just then Gary saw her and waved. As she closed the gate behind her she looked up to see where the stranger had got to, and saw he was striding off beside the hedge, already thirty yards away.

'Have you come for Tony?' asked Gary. He did not sound very put out about it. 'We just took a bit of a tumble back there ...' he nodded back up the track where Tony was still sitting roaring among the bales '... but I think he's okay. You all right, Tony?' he added, perfunctorily. Fish was bending over him trying to look helpful, but when Tony saw Ruth his wails increased.

'I want Mom,' he howled. 'I want my Mom.'

The other boys shifted uncomfortably. Chivalry dictated that, in the circumstances, they must allow Tony his private weapon, but chivalry was beginning to wane a little.

'Shut up, Tony, and come on,' said Ruth mechanically.

'I didn't get my proper turn,' said Tony. 'It's not fair.'

'We did,' said Gary. 'If we didn't make it that's our look-out.'

'We'll just have our turn while you're recovering, and then

18

it will be your turn anyway,' said Jimmy. 'If he hasn't got to go at once, that is,' he added to Ruth.

But this merely served to enrage Tony more than ever, and he claimed hotly the right to have another run straightaway. In the end the other boys agreed, obviously only because that was the easiest way to get rid of him.

'O.K.,' said Jimmy. 'You two go next and then we'll go after, since you've got to go home now.'

'No, I don't,' said Tony, but the others ignored that.

'We'll all have to go home, anyway,' said Fish, not very convincingly.

Ruth watched while they had their run, Tony telling Gary to be more careful and not make a mess of it, and they descended sedately and without incident and Jimmy said he hadn't timed it properly but it was a jolly good run, quite likely the best yet. As Ruth led Tony away across the field she heard the others happily planning a more testing route for solo descents. It did not sound as though they were all just about to go home.

'You mustn't be such a baby,' said Ruth.

'I want Mom,' said Tony.

Suddenly Ruth stopped short. That's all we ever say to each other, she thought. Perhaps it's my fault. I never expect him to understand.

'Tony,' she said, carefully keeping her voice humble, 'I do, too. Don't you see that?'

'It's okay for you. You're older,' said Tony unconcernedly. 'Come on.'

'If you weren't so darned full of yourself ...' Ruth began furiously, but she did not finished the sentence. What was the use? She could have hit him, shaken him, anything to make him aware of her as a person who could have feelings too, but she knew that, if she did so, Tony would run crying home to tell Auntie Mary, leaving Ruth too proud to deny it and too shy to explain it.

She made no effort to catch Tony up. He had broken into a run and was already by the gate into the garden when Pete met him there. Evidently he was asking for Ruth, because Tony gave a casual wave in her direction and disappeared towards the house. Pete came straight on towards her, and immediately she knew there must be some news. Pete was always polite and companionable when circumstances threw them together, but he was not exactly forthcoming. Ruth accepted that. Lots of people, boys especially, felt that way about her, as though they did not know how to talk to her. Now, when she saw him coming quickly across the field, she knew he must have been sent to find her.

'Hi, Pete,' she called, with a slightly false heartiness.

'Hi,' said Pete. Whatever it was he had come to say, he did not want to shout it across the field, for he just kept on coming. Then at last he spoke.

'The hospital have just rung, about Patsy. She's better, she's regained consciousness.'

'Really better?'

I must smile, thought Ruth, he'll expect me to smile, to look happy, but this feeling that's in my chest somewhere, it hasn't got anything to do with my lips. Something must be made to go on outside while my whole being breaks into flower inside me.

'That's what they say. She's been talking, and asking for you, and Auntie Sybil, of course . . .'

'Does she know about Dad?'

'I don't know.'

'I must go see her.' Ruth began to walk on quickly, but her legs felt weak.

'That's all right, that's all fixed up,' said Pete.

'They'll let me go?'

'I don't think they would have, only that Auntie Sybil's in hospital.'

'When? Now?'

'When Uncle Sam comes off duty – that's in about half-an-hour – he'll take you down, and Mum, so Dad and I can stay and look after Tony. I don't suppose he'll like it much, but they won't let him in.'

'Oh, Tony can go fry,' said Ruth, and found she was smiling, laughing even, or was it crying? 'Oh, Pete, is she really better? She's not lost her memory, or paralysed or anything?' These were the fears she had thought she could never tell anyone, but Pete just stood there, quiet and attentive – like his father, Ruth thought suddenly.

'It's only what the message from the hospital said,' Pete explained. 'It didn't seem like it – well on the way to recovery, or something like that, was what they said. You'll know more when you see her.' Ruth remained silent; had she been jubilant too soon?

'Sit down a minute,' said Pete unexpectedly. 'You look a bit funny. There's no hurry,' he added, stretching himself on his tummy on the ground. 'You can't go till Uncle Sam comes in.' For a moment he chewed a piece of grass, watching Ruth as she sat hugging her knees. Then he said, 'Knowing Patsy, she'll be all right. You can't imagine her doing anything by halves, can you?'

'No,' said Ruth, 'no.'

Gradually she uncurled, her whole body relaxing until she was lying flat on the grass, her arms stretched as far above her head as they would go, and the evening August sun shining warm on her body.

After a while, Pete spoke, without looking up from the grasses he was studying a few inches from his nose.

'You know what you said this afternoon? You meant Patsy, didn't you?'

'I was just being silly,' said Ruth. 'I didn't really mean it.'

'I would have,' said Pete. 'If I'd thought she wasn't going to get better.'

Ruth was shamed. 'Well, I guess I did then,' she said. 'But I don't now.' Pete did not answer, and after a moment Ruth went on. It was easy to talk like this, lying in the sunshine with her eyes closed. Pete was silent and invisible, and the gap between thinking to herself and talking to someone else had never seemed so narrow, except of course with Patsy.

'It was seeing her in hospital,' she said. 'She wasn't like a person – more like a thing. You know what Patsy is like normally. Of course, you haven't seen her this time, have you? Only when we were over, two years ago. I don't think she's changed much since then. You were always fighting, I remember. Patsy loved it.'

Pete rolled over and sat up. 'We'd better go in,' he said. 'Uncle Sam will be home soon. What do you think I can do to keep Tony happy?'

'Don't ask me,' said Ruth, getting to her feet. 'Whatever you do you'll be better at it than I am. Patsy's the only one who can do anything with him. She even seems to like him.'

'He's not that bad,' said Pete, laughing. 'We'll think of something.'

'It must be terrible for you, all this,' said Ruth. 'Turned out of your own house and everything, and getting landed with all the worst jobs.'

'I'll survive,' said Pete. He pulled open the garden gate. 'As a matter of fact, it's probably just as well Mum's not got time to think about me. I was expecting trouble from her when I got back from Scotland.'

'Why?'

'Oh, it's a long story. She thought I was going to Germany with the school, and there was a bit of a mix-up about me being in with some other boys breaking the law about something, and the Head wouldn't let me go. I didn't want to tell Mum about it, so I just kept the money and went to see Dad instead.'

'Do you know, I thought there was something funny going on. Your Mom was being terrifically cagey about you, con-

22

sidering how they talk usually, your Mom and mine.' She looked at him uncertainly, wondering whether he would think her nosy if she asked him to tell her the whole story, or unfriendly if she didn't. Patsy would have asked, straightaway.

She was still wondering when they reached the back door and Pete, infected by her silence, was silent, too.

'What did ...?' began Ruth, but at that moment Auntie Mary appeared at the back door, smiling.

'Pete told you the good news?' she said.

Chapter 2

IT was several days later, when Ruth had gone for a walk up the stream that ran along the valley marking the boundary of the Thomases' land, that she remembered she had never asked anybody about the strange man she had met leaning on the gate.

There had been plenty of other things to think about. It was extraordinary how quickly she and everybody else in the family had come to accept the change in Patsy's situation. Only a few days ago her name was scarcely mentioned though the thought of her lay like lead on the household. Now the conversation dealt casually with the ordinary everyday problems of visiting her and taking her clean night-clothes and games to play. That first evening when Ruth went to see her she was, not unnaturally, pale and puzzled but already making good friends out of the nurses. By the next day she had been moved into the main ward and had obviously become the life and soul of the place.

After that first occasion, Ruth and her aunt took it in turns to visit Patsy, driven over either by Pete's father or by Uncle Sam, and though the hospital was anxious to keep her under observation for a few more days it soon became clear that it would not be long before Patsy would be allowed home. As Mrs Jenkins left off worrying about Patsy she became increasingly concerned about her sister, alone in Bristol and shortly to have an operation. She did get over to see her one day after visiting Patsy, and Uncle Jack took Ruth to see her mother another day, but these visits did not seem to offer much in the way of company for her. When Ruth was there she had difficulty in finding things to talk about. It seemed so strange to see Mom lying doing nothing, waiting to be talked to; it made her seem like a different person. Yes, she said, of course they were okay, yes, Tony was fine, yes, it was terrific that Patsy was getting on so well; and that seemed to be all there was to say.

Mrs Jenkins explained to her about the operation. It was something internal they had not been able to do until she was strong enough.

'It's not serious, I suppose,' said Mrs Jenkins to Ruth after she got back from the long drive to Bristol, 'but she'll be ever so lonely down there by herself. I was wondering whether maybe you could manage here if I went and stayed there to be with her for a few days. If I go now, your uncle will be at home' – Uncle Jack still had another week of his holiday before returning to his road-building job in Scotland – 'and I thought maybe you and Pete could look after yourselves and Tony – and then I'll be back for when they send Patsy home from hospital.'

'Of course,' said Ruth, but she felt suddenly alarmed. She was not afraid the household would collapse; she knew that Uncle Jack in his silent imperturbable way would sweep the stairs and lay the table and see that no one went hungry, and she knew that Pete was surprisingly good, in a casual sort of way, at frying sausages or scrambling eggs. What worried her was that it was she who ought to be able to do all those sort of things, and she couldn't.

Ruth's mother was one of those housewives to whom perfection came as easily as leaves to a tree; she cleaned and cooked and mended with the same joyful concentration that an artist lavishes upon his painting, and allowed her daughters to help with about as much enthusiasm as an artist would welcome the assistance of his children bringing their crayons to finish off his masterpiece. It never bothered Ruth, who at any time would have much preferred to read a book than to fry an egg, and anyhow she was further discouraged by Patsy's experience. Patsy really did feel the urge to help, and thoroughly enjoyed being domesticated, but her well-meant efforts always ended in angry scenes with Patsy complaining that her mother was never satisfied and her mother declaring she was only trying to show her how to do the thing properly.

As a result, Ruth removed herself discreetly from the domestic scene, and had happily reached the age of fourteen without ever doing anything more taxing than making her bed – and in fact had only discovered during the past week how uncomfortable a bed could get if nobody came by with smoothing hands between her making it in the morning and getting into it at night.

Since the disaster, deprived of both her mother and Patsy to shield her incompetence, Ruth had found herself in a difficult position. For very shame she could not bring herself to tell Auntie Mary that she did not know how to set about the kind of chores her aunt took it for granted she could do, and yet she did not want to appear uncooperative. She took to keeping out of the way or pretending to be lost in a book or in her own thoughts, aware that her aunt, harassed by the crisis, must think her pretty useless.

She wasn't even, she reflected, much good at amusing Tony. Since the evening when she and her aunt had gone down to see Patsy that first time, leaving Pete to look after Tony, her young brother had taken to following Pete everywhere like a puppy. It was very convenient, as long as Pete was good-humouredly prepared to take him around with him, but it left Ruth with even less excuse for not taking over the household duties when her aunt went off to Bristol.

As usual at times like this, Ruth decided to take herself out for a walk.

She went out through the little gate at the end of the garden into the field behind the house, but instead of cutting across the upper part of it towards Tygwyn farm, where she had gone to fetch Tony, she turned right and followed the slope of the meadow down to the stream that ran along the bottom. Here, if she went downstream, she would soon arrive back in the village, where the little bridge separated the main village from the school and church. Ruth did not want to do that, though, so she wandered along upstream, where the ground was tussocky and hard between the alders now in August, but most of the year was boggy and churned up by the cows. She passed the old stone barn, full of the new season's hay cut a few weeks earlier from the meadow, and soon afterwards came to another bridge where the narrow lane that cut down past Tygwyn crossed the stream and wound up into the hills on the other side. After the first mile the hedgerows petered out into a few straggling and stunted thorn trees and the sheep by the roadside scampered suddenly into the green fern. The fingers of the bracken itself ran out towards the upper lip of the gully, and above that all was open grassland and wide blue views. Ruth wondered whether she had time and perseverance to make the long pull up to that rounded skyline. The last time she had been there was a fortnight ago when her father had driven them all up for a family picnic.

Here in Wales, where her mother had her roots and the old network of relationships ran like lace through the neighbouring villages, her father seemed diminished; from being an arbitrary god he became an uneasy chauffeur and hanger-on. Ruth found him altogether more likeable, and she remembered that on that day in the hills while her mother and Auntie Mary peacefully reigned over the picnic basket and Patsy supervised an assortment of small boys playing in the stream, she had walked with him to the top of the long ridge above them and gazed down at the patchwork panorama of green and tawny fields. They had not talked to each other much, but Ruth had felt less impatient of his presence than she usually did.

She decided not to go up there again today, but to follow the brook upstream. She had never explored that way before, so there would be no memories to try and forget.

At first the stream ran through fields as it had done before, but they tended to be smaller and rougher, and Ruth had to skirt around a good many boggy patches. On the opposite side, the hill began to fall more steeply to the bank, until she was walking under the shadow of a hanging oak wood. After another half mile the brook curved round the foot of the ridge, and led away from the open farmland into a narrow valley that headed up into the steep flank of the mountains. Here the straggling line of alders that had clung to Ruth's side of the stream spread out to form a rough spinney covering the whole neck of the valley; the air was rich with the smells of moist peat and rotting wood and wild mint. As Ruth worked her way to higher ground to avoid the bogs, the alders began to give way to sycamores and a few massive oaks, themselves supporting a little world of greenery in their ancient forks, where sapling trees and ferns and huge lobed fungi sucked life from the crumbling wood. Underfoot, bracken and brambles grew thinly, and the ground between was carpeted with the shining leaves and pale seedheads of last June's bluebells. It was a primeval untrodden place, unlike anything Ruth had seen before. There were birds innumerable and unterrified in the great branches, and a variety of burrows among the bluebell leaves. Ruth did not know what they all were, but she tried to notice details so that she could ask Pete. He was an enthusiast about birds, and would probably know whether badger, fox or rabbit had made these brown scars in the greenery.

She began to climb upwards, wondering how far this neglected woodland extended, but she was brought to an abrupt halt by a strongly-made wire fence running straight and taut across the hillside. Right up to the fence life reigned in disorganized abundance under the ancient oaks, but beyond it straight ranks of firs marched starkly across unheeded contours and below each dark tunnel the earth hibernated under a pall of pine needles.

Ruth followed the fence for a short distance, and then turned away from the sombre plantation to plunge back into the wilderness. Then she stopped, startled. Before her stood an old shack, an ancient corrugated-iron structure used by foresters or roadmen, long since abandoned and already half-absorbed into the landscape, rusty and askew, draped in honeysuckle and brambles and hidden by sapling hazels. It was not so much the building itself that surprised her, but the smell. Over and above the musty smell of rotting leaves and the tang of wild mint there was the familiar and unmistakable smell of Sunday dinner. It carried so vivid a picture of plates round the family table steaming with meat and roast potatoes and green peas and gravy that a pang of pure hunger overtook Ruth's first sensation of surprise, quickly doused by a feeling of alarm. She glanced around, noting the unhurried smoke filtering up through the branches beyond the shack, the string tied across between two trees, the brushwood piled against the back of the building, the old tarpaulin covering something on the far side of the clearing and the enamel bowl lying on the ground. Somebody must live in this unlikely spot.

Almost at once, Ruth felt she knew who it was. The knowledge came to her so quickly that when, in that instant, she saw the man standing quietly watching her, grey-green as the wild mint and umber as the rotting leaves, she recognized him with no surprise. It was the man she had met leaning on the gate at Tygwyn watching the boys at play.

He nodded at Ruth casually and went on walking towards the far side of the hut, in the direction of the smoke. Ruth took a few cautious steps forward to see where he had gone and found him turning a stick with some sort of meat skewered on it over the glowing ashes of his fire. An ancient blackened pot nestled in the ashes alongside.

'You got a dog?' he asked over his shoulder.

'I beg your pardon?' said Ruth, puzzled by the abrupt question.

'Not got no dog with you, have you?'

'No, I haven't. Why?'

'It's best to be sure.' He lifted the lid of the pot and sniffed the steam. 'Should be done soon,' he added. 'Not that I've got anything against dogs. Used always to have one as a boy.' He got up and studied her carefully. 'It's the hedgehogs I'm thinking about, see.'

'Hedgehogs?'

'Be all right if they was big. A grown hedgehog's more than a match for a dog, any day.' He scratched his stubbly chin. 'I don't suppose you've got a mug or a bowl or something like that?'

'No, I haven't,' said Ruth, bemused.

'I'll see what I've got,' he said and disappeared inside the shack.

Ruth hovered, wondering whether to take the opportunity to escape. She was less alarmed now she knew it was just the old man she had met before but she still felt a little apprehensive. 'Gee, weren't you scared?' the girls back in New York would say if she told them. 'I'd have run a mile.'

But she wouldn't be seeing the girls in New York, perhaps not ever again. All that was dead and gone. If she could not go back, then she must go forward, or live in a land of ghosts for ever.

She walked up to the fire-place and, with the smell of wood-smoke and roasting meat in her nostrils, peered in through the dark doorway of the shed.

'What did you mean about the hedgehogs?' she asked.

The man was scuffling about in the dim interior and did not answer. He probably hadn't heard, Ruth thought, and examined the lump of meat on the stick. It was getting rather black on the underside, and spurts of flame kept licking up out of the embers where the fat dripped on to them. She carefully turned the stick over, wondering about the little carcase. Hedgehog? she thought, suddenly dismayed.

The man came stooping out of the shack, carrying an enamel bowl and, unexpectedly, a tinfoil dish that must once have come from a supermarket freezer.

'Thought I might find summat like this if I looked,' he said with satisfaction, laying the dishes down by the fire. 'Come on then, and I'll show you.' He moved off among the trees.

'Show me what?' asked Ruth. All her careful middle-class upbringing cried out to her not to follow disreputable strangers into lonely woods. She followed, but at a cautious distance.

'Where I've got 'em,' he said, and waited for her to catch up. She had to come up to him then, but he did not seem to notice her hesitation, and just turned and walked on through the trees, talking as he went.

'It's the traffic,' he said. 'Terrible lot get killed that way. As soon as she didn't come three nights ago, I knew she'd gone. I went up the lane to look, and saw the old owl fly up off the road. That'll be her, I thought, and it was. Flat as a pancake, of course.'

'The hedgehog?' said Ruth.

'Aye, the old 'un. She was getting on, mind. Been around my place a fair while.'

'Was she a pet hedgehog, then? Was she yours, I mean?'

'No, she wasn't mine. I don't own nothing like that. The wood's she was, like me. It's just we'd got a bit friendly, like, over the years. Come round my fire most evenings, she would, and often I'd hear her, if I waked in the night, rustling around outside – inside, sometimes, if she thought she'd find something to eat there.' He stopped by a straggle of brambles sprawling over a bank. 'Down by here, they are.'

He suddenly put a strong hand on Ruth's shoulder and for a rigid moment panic stabbed her. But his whole attention was focused, childlike, upon his treasure. As he gently flattened the drift of dead leaves with his free hand he pressed her down with the other till she could see right into the hollow scooped out beneath the bramble roots. It seemed at first glance to be full of burrs, but then she realized they were a clutch of baby hedgehogs.

'Feel 'em,' he said, 'but don't wake 'em. They'll be wanting to feed, else, and it's a long time yet till dusk.'

Ruth put her hand nervously into the hollow, and to her surprise the spines were soft, like the green fuzz on unripe sweet chestnuts. They were warm, and softly heaving up and down in the deep breathing of sleep.

She withdrew her hand and stood up, and the man carefully stirred up the leaves to cover the mouth of the hole.

'Mustn't let the old fox get 'em,' he said, and turned back towards his home.

'How did you know they were there?' asked Ruth. She had lost all fear of him now.

'Oh, I knew where she'd got 'em all right,' he said. 'Somewhere round that patch of brambles she makes her nest, every year, and I'd seen her, scuffing up the leaves over the hole, more 'n once.'

'Have you been feeding them, then, since she was killed?'

'Oh, aye, I puts milk out for 'em, night and morning, and a few scraps of meat and that. But they find their own food, too. They're getting they'll be able to look after themselves by the autumn, if the fox keeps away. Till their spines harden, they ain't no match for a fox, nor a dog.' They had reached the clearing, and for a time the old man just stood staring at the fire. 'They won't all come through the winter, of course,' he said. 'But maybe there'll be one of 'em that'll keep coming around here for scraps in the summer evenings, same as the old 'n. Company, she were.'

He took the lid off the pan and ladled vegetable stew into the two dishes. Suddenly Ruth realized why he had asked her if she had a bowl. Then he produced a sheath-knife from his

32

pocket and eased the meat off its stick and laid it on a flat stone to cut it in half.

'Fond of pigeon?' he asked.

So that's what it was, thought Ruth, relieved. 'I've never had any,' she said. 'I expect so, but I mustn't eat your dinner. I'll be getting mine when I go home.'

'It's nice,' he said. 'Real tasty.' He looked up at her hopefully. 'It's all wholesome,' he said, 'and there's plenty here. More than enough for two.' Then, as she still hesitated, 'Go on,' he added, 'you can eat two dinners. You needn't tell 'em at home about this one. Look, I've put it all out for you.' He pulled the big bent spoon out of the pot and laid it in the tinfoil dish. 'There you are; spoon and all. You sit down there and eat it.'

'How are you going to manage, if I have your spoon?' said Ruth, but she had already decided to follow this thing through, and was sitting down by the fireside.

'I'll manage, don't you worry,' said the man. 'And I've got my knife.'

A knife did not seem the easiest instrument for eating stew with but the man managed quite comfortably by holding the bowl to his mouth as though he were drinking from it and using the knife to propel the solid bits in. It was a great deal more effective than a spoon when it came to spit-roasted pigeon, and after a brief endeavour to be genteel, Ruth took the carcase in her hand and pulled the meat off with her teeth, which, since her host was doing the same thing, she assumed would pass as normal etiquette.

The pigeon tasted strange and smoky, but delicious. The stew was less interesting than it smelt, being watery and unsalted, but the vegetables floating about in it were reassuringly recognizable as turnip and potato and onion.

'How do you manage to live?' asked Ruth at last. Now she had eaten with him she felt able to ask the obvious question. 'I mean, getting your food and that?'

'Maybe I do a bit of poaching now and again,' he said. 'But not so's anyone worries. Pigeons, now, you can shoot 'em where you please, and no one minds. The farmers give me turnips and potatoes and that. Maybe I do the odd job, harvesting or shearing-time, and they say to go and help myself from the clamp. A sack of turnips lasts a long time. Onions, now, that's different. John's wife mostly gives me them. She knows I likes a bit of onion in the stew.'

Ruth wondered who John's wife was, but did not want to seem too inquisitive, so she let it pass. There were other questions she wanted to ask that were more important.

'Do you always live here?' she asked. 'Winter and all?'

'Sometimes I do,' he said. 'If they let me. But John's wife don't like it, so I takes to the road, mostly, comes the winter, case they get me shut up some place. I go to the towns then. Tried one of them hostels one year, but that weren't much cop, I don't want to try that again, not until I have to. How old would you think I was?'

Ruth sensed a catch here. Grown-ups were funny about their ages; sometimes they wanted you to think they were older than they were, and sometimes younger, but whichever it was they always wanted you to be wrong, so that they could surprise you.

'Sixty,' she said at random. She could tell by his disappointed face that she had made a mistake and guessed right. 'No,' she said, quickly. 'I was only kidding. I should say you are forty-seven.'

'I am sixty,' he said. 'But you'd never have guessed it, would you? I don't look my age, I know that. It's the open-air life. But don't you go telling anyone, or they'll be putting me in one of them old people's homes.'

'Who's they?' asked Ruth. 'John's wife?'

'Funny you should say that,' said the man. 'Do you think she would?'

'I don't know,' said Ruth.

'It'd be awkward, that,' he said. He gazed over the rim of

the bowl, unmoving, while he considered. Then he shook his head and went on eating. 'I don't think she would, you know,' he added with his mouth full. 'It would be the devil if she did, though.'

'Why?'

'I reckon she must know my age, very near, 'cos of John.'

'Does John know?'

'He's my brother, see. Two years younger, and a lot sharper when we was in school together.'

Ruth tried to picture him in school, one among the little scrubbed boys packed like sardines behind bench desks in the village school, and fed on the arid text-book diet of fifty years ago. Did he come to school with hedgehogs in his pockets? she wondered.

'No,' the man was saying, 'I don't think John's wife would get me shut up. The police it is, or the men from the Council. They don't like people not living tidy in houses.'

'Thank you for the dinner,' said Ruth, who had finished. 'I think I'd better be getting back.' She remembered the house-work problem awaiting her. 'How do you do the dishes?' she asked, looking at the greasy plate in her hand.

'Oh, aye, we can do them proper today, seeing as the stew is finished,' said the man, getting up. 'Come along, and I'll show you.' He gathered up the blackened empty pan that had held the stew and moved off through the woods with it. Ruth followed, still clutching her dish.

Before they had gone many steps she could hear the sound of splashing water, and came upon a patch of bog, bright with water plants. An old piece of guttering stuck out of a bank over it, and the clear water fell from the broken end and lost itself in the moist earth.

'Where does it come from?' asked Ruth curiously, as the old man held his pot under the trickle and waited patiently for it to fill.

'Must be a bit of a spring somewhere up there,' he said

35

unconcernedly. 'Beautiful water it is, and don't often dry up.'

'What do you do when it does?'

'Have to go down to the brook, then,' he said, nodding down the valley. 'Or go without.' He turned and walked back to the fire, Ruth still following with her dish, and set the pan carefully among the red-hot embers.

'I used to have another pot,' he said regretfully. 'It were easier then – one for the stew and one to hot the water. But it went into a great hole, so I put it under the bank, and there's robins nested in it this year, so it hasn't gone to waste.'

'How do you do the dishes if you haven't finished the stew?' said Ruth. This was housekeeping at a simple level and even Ruth felt she could keep her end up in the conversation.

'I wait till I have,' said the man, and there was a certain logical simplicity about that, too, Ruth thought.

'It's lucky you're not married to my mother,' she said, giggling, and then pulled herself up short, surprised and a little shocked by her own openness. It was a Patsy remark, and made to anyone else would have led to the kind of banter that Ruth would not have known how to deal with. Her companion, however, responded with childlike simplicity.

'Is she very clean, then?' he asked, his blue eyes anxious. 'About the washing-up and that?' He shook his head. 'My mother was. And John's wife. I suppose that's why I never married.'

Ruth felt she had rebuked him, and cast around for something solacing to say.

'I don't suppose the hedgehogs mind,' she said. On an impulse she added, 'I must go now, but can I come again and see them?'

'Aye, aye, you come when you want to. Maybe your brother would like to come and see the hedgehogs? Him with the fair hair, that's timid?'

Ruth wasn't at all sure she wanted to let Tony into it. She had fallen into a little adventure of her own, and she felt she would like to keep it that way, at least until Patsy was well enough to come with her.

'Thank you,' she said, 'I'm sure he would love it, but he's often with the other boys.' She sensed the old man would not want a gang of rowdy children invading his hide-out, and she was right.

'Boys together ain't no use,' he said, 'not in the woods. All right for a game' – Ruth remembered how he had enjoyed the go-cart racing – 'but no good in the woods. Can't stop making a racket, not unless you get one on his own.'

Ruth reflected that Tony could keep up a fair racket even when on his own, and resolved not to tell him anything about it. She thanked her host politely for the stew, and set off back through the dingle.

Chapter 3

NEXT morning, Ruth woke up inspired with domestic zeal. If a simple-minded old man living in the woods could master the basic essentials of housekeeping, then so could she. For the first time in her life, she realized that cooking and cleaning and making and mending did not necessarily have to be performed at the level of perfection practised by her mother in order to be worth doing at all. To her mother, frying an egg badly was an affront to the art of cookery, in the same way that a ballet dancer clumping through a *pas de seul* was an affront to the art of ballet – if you couldn't do the thing well, then you shouldn't be seen doing it at all.

That was the wrong way to look at it, Ruth decided, because only dancers need dance, but everybody had to eat if they were not to starve, and keep themselves clothed if they were not to freeze, and no one could count on having a perfectionist mother always in the offing. She had discovered that for herself in the past two weeks. Now she came to think of it, even Auntie Mary, who ran her mother close in the housekeeping stakes, managed to get by without always doing everything that her mother would have considered necessary: vegetables sometimes came straight to the table in the saucepan, and she contented herself with saying to Ruth, 'You can keep your own bedroom tidy, dear, can't you?' without coming in later on to check that it was. Ruth ran her finger across the surface of her bedside table, noted the grey dust clinging to it and hastily picked up her nightie and used it to give the table a careful rub. She then gave her nightie a good shake, and seeing the motes hovering in the morning sunshine as it slanted through her bedroom window and settling back on the table again, she thought: so that's why housewives shake dusters out of windows. It was a ritual she had always taken for granted, just part of the mysterious art of housekeeping, without ever really questioning its purpose.

When she got downstairs, Pete and his father were getting the breakfast. Patsy, if she had made a resolve to be domesticated, would have rushed upon them like a whirlwind and taken over every job that was going, but that was not Ruth's way. Instead, she stood quietly by the window, apparently in one of her usual dreams, but in fact watching them carefully. Pete was laying rashers of bacon in the hot frying-pan and licking his fingers absent-mindedly between each piece. His father was laying the table.

'Table-cloth's a bit mucky,' he said, studying a patch where Tony has spilt the ketchup at supper-time. 'Shall we do without, or put the cornflakes packet on it?' He was asking Ruth, with a slow smile, as though they were all in this together. Then the thought must have struck him that perhaps she was not one of them, after all, but, as befitted her sex, a member of the other camp. 'Perhaps we'd better have a clean one,' he said. 'Pete, do you know where your mother keeps the clean cloths?'

'Oh, no,' said Ruth. 'It only makes more washing for her when she comes back.'

'Sure?' said Uncle Jack, fetching the cornflakes packet, and placing it carefully over the stain. 'Looks all right, don't it?'

'Fine,' said Ruth. 'I'll fill up the sugar basin.' She had noticed, in her new-found enthusiasm, that it was nearly empty, and had been wondering how to find out where the sugar packet was kept without having to betray her ignorance by asking, when she had observed it alongside the cereals in the cupboard. A small victory, but a victory nonetheless.

'I could do a spot of washing,' said Uncle Jack. 'I promised Sam I'd be up at the field at ten, to help with fixing them gates for the rodeo, but if I'm there punctual I'll bet I'll be the only one that is.'

'I'll do the washing,' said Ruth. 'I haven't anything else to do. You and Pete have got plenty to do up at the field today. Didn't you say you were helping up there all day, Pete?'

'Yeah, and me too,' said Tony, coming downstairs with his hair on end and his pullover back to front.

'Much use you'll be,' said Ruth, and then wished she hadn't.

'I expect all the kids will be up there, running around,' said Uncle Jack. 'Tony won't come to no harm.'

'I'm going with Pete,' said Tony. 'We have to set the bales out, don't we?'

'You come along,' said Pete. 'I don't know as you can actually shift the bales – they're pretty heavy, really – but you can mess about with Gary and Fish and the others.'

'I'm helping you,' said Tony, and nobody bothered to argue the point.

The next day the Llanwern annual Agricultural Show was to take place. To the casual motorist passing by and seeing a couple of faded marquees over the top of the hedge, and a few stock-lorries lurching down Thomas's lane, it would appear a pretty small affair, but it was a big event in the life of Llanwern, and entailed a lot of preparation for most of its inhabitants. The farmers and the boys would be out in the big top field that lay between Tygwyn and the main road, the one where the boys played football because it was the only flat field in the neighbourhood, driving in posts to fence off a main ring, fixing sheep and cattle-pens, setting up trestles and booths, and deciding who was to be in charge of what.

As the older men chewed over the problems of seeing that no job was without a man, and no man who expected a job should be without one, and that the jobs left for the sons and nephews should not exceed in status the jobs reserved for the fathers and uncles, the older boys possessed themselves of the axes and sledgehammers resting in their idle hands and the rough hanks of baler twine tumbling out of the backs of land-rovers and strode off to set the field to rights.

'Is there anything I should be doing?' asked Ruth, over the bacon Pete had cooked. 'I mean for the Show?' She had no idea what, since she had never experienced a village Show, but everyone seemed to be doing something, even Tony.

'Mum usually helps with the refreshments,' said Pete. 'Up at Tygwyn, cutting sandwiches and that. But that's on the day – I don't think she does much the day before. Makes some cakes, probably.'

Ruth's heart sank. She was prepared to have a go with a cookery book while the others were all out, but only for their family consumption. She did not fancy going up to Tygwyn with a poor little flat and leathery cake to set beside Mrs Thomas's sumptuous billowing sponges. However, Tony came to her rescue unexpectedly.

'Auntie Mary made some cakes before she went. I took them over to Tygwyn for her yesterday. Oh, yeah, and Mrs Thomas told me to tell you to go over there if you'd finished up here, to help with the Show.'

'When?' said Ruth. 'You never said.'

'I forgot,' said Tony unconcernedly. 'You were out when I came back. Gone for a walk or something dumb.' That would have been the day before, when she had met the old man in the wood. 'Anyway, what's it matter? I guess she didn't really want you to help. She just thought you might be bored without any other girls around. Come on, Pete, let's get up to the field.'

Pete looked at him rather coolly. 'You go, if you want to,' he said. 'I'll be along in a few minutes. Ruth and I have the washing-up to do.' It was a gentle rebuff, and slid off Tony, but Ruth was grateful to him, not for offering to do the dishes, but for dissociating himself from Tony's bid to exclude her from this boys' club.

'*I'll* do the dishes,' she said. She looked across at Uncle Jack, carefully stacking the breakfast things ready to take over to the sink. 'Leave them,' she said. 'If you all go on up to the field I'll have the morning to myself here and maybe I'll be able to produce you some sort of dinner. I'd really like to do that. I can manage okay if I'm on my own.'

Uncle Jack looked at her doubtfully. 'All right,' he said. 'And if you get tired of your own company, you slip over to Tygwyn. The girls will be glad to see you, shouldn't wonder. There's a pie of some sort your aunt left in the fridge, so you needn't worry about getting no dinner.'

After they had gone, Ruth set about the washing-up enthusiastically. As she piled the wet things on the draining-board she decided she wasn't going to be content just to dish up Auntie Mary's pie; she could cook a proper hot dinner for Pete and his father to come home to. She looked around for a cookery book and eventually found an ancient tattered paperback at the bottom of a drawer. She began to read the recipes but became increasingly puzzled that every one should contain a commodity she had never even heard of, called Karo. It must be something very common in Britain, since it appeared to be an essential ingredient of so many dishes, and in quite large quantities, too – half a pound here, six ounces there, a whole pound in the next one. Ruth began to search the store cupboard for Karo, but there was none to be found; she looked in the fridge and the vegetable rack and wondered whether she ought to study the vegetable garden and the fruit trees but realized she would not recognize it even if it *was* growing there.

Exploring the store cupboard was quite a fascinating occupation and Ruth spent a long time happily sniffing and prodding and occasionally tasting. The big flour tin seemed to take pride of place and it was odd, now that she came to think about it, that none of the recipes she had read in the cook-book seemed

42

to use flour. Another study of the book confirmed this impression – flour was not mentioned once – and yet all the recipes seemed to concern various kinds of cakes and breads. She decided to see if she could find a less confusing recipe book.

Deeper burrowing at the back of the drawer finally produced a collection of crumpled cuttings from various magazines with headings like 'Fish with a Difference' and 'Party Fare for Children' and a single sheet that had obviously been the front cover of the cook-book. Turning it over to discover the title of the book, Ruth read: *The Karo Self-Raising Flour Book of Plain Cookery.*

Light dawned; but her problem was not wholly solved. How was she to find out whether Auntie Mary's flour was Karo? and if not, did it matter? Anyway, she thought, Uncle Jack won't want cake for his main course at dinner; he'll want chops, or stew, or cottage pie.

Since the Karo cookery book did not concern itself with meat and vegetables, Ruth turned her attention to the cuttings. She decided the fish dish looked easy to prepare, and went back to wiping the cutlery dry, satisfied that she had got the meal planned out, till she realized there probably would not be any fish in the house. She abandoned the knives and forks to have a look and discovered she was right. Fish was not the kind of food likely to be lying around the cupboard on the off-chance that it might come in useful, and the same was obviously true of meat, so that the recipe which began with raw minced steak was not going to be any use either.

It occurred to her that she might get on better if she took stock of what *was* available first, and then hunted for a recipe to suit the ingredients. Apart from the cold meat pie – which looked delicious but Ruth was determined to abjure it – there were eggs and sausages and bacon and some tins of baked beans and spaghetti, and lots of potatoes, brought in from the garden yesterday by Uncle Jack.

They're sure to want potatoes, she thought. They always

did. Pete had a limitless capacity for potatoes. It seemed a good idea to get the potatoes peeled while deciding what else to cook. It might also have been sensible to have dried the remaining breakfast dishes first and put them away, but Ruth did not think of that until she discovered them all splashed with earthy potato water and spattered with peelings, so she had to wash the dishes all over again. Meantime the half-peeled potatoes had begun to turn brown, and peeling a saucepanful took her a very long time.

Not that Ruth was particularly conscious of the passage of time, being quite happy peacefully teaching herself this new skill, until she heard children's voices in the lane outside the house.

'Come *on*,' the older one was saying to his dawdling little sister, 'or we'll be late for dinner and Mummy will be cross.'

Ruth glanced panic-stricken at the clock and saw it was twelve o'clock. It was lucky Uncle Jack and Pete would not be expecting a punctual dinner, but it was sobering to find that it had taken her over two hours just to wash up the breakfast and peel a few potatoes. Cold pie? No. Ruth was not prepared to admit defeat yet, and rushed back to the recipe cuttings. Luck was with her. The first one she picked up told her how to make something called Friday Pie (it *is* Friday, too, she thought) and it required eggs, bacon, tomatoes, cheese, flour and lard. She knew from her investigations that all those things were in the house, so she set to with renewed confidence.

She found that mixing the pastry was rather fun, and she crumbled meticulously until the fat and flour, according to instructions, were like fine bread-crumbs. Adding the water and kneading the dough into a ball was fascinating, too; Ruth was as happy as a four-year-old in a sandpit until she began to run into trouble rolling it out. It seemed to have a persistent knack of sticking to the table, or sticking to the rolling-pin, or pulling into holes; she did not dare look at the clock until she had the pie-dish lined with what was by now a somewhat trampled-looking substance and filled with the layers of chopped bacon and tomato and grated cheese.

Then, when she went to fetch the eggs, she looked at the time and was horrified to see it was ten to one. Where had the time gone to? Never mind, it was almost ready for the oven now, and maybe the others would be kept late on the field.

Late or no, it was with a feeling of pride that she carried the completed pie across to the electric cooker – only to realize that the oven was stone cold.

It was then Ruth discovered, to her surprise, that a simple housekeeping disappointment could more effectively reduce her to tears than the most baffling of Latin unseens or mathematical problems. Only pride and an awareness of the family's imminent return prevented her from running upstairs to fling herself upon her bed, sobbing for a world of unknown things as well as a cold oven.

Instead she stood still in the kitchen, staring mistily at the saucepanful of potatoes until it came into focus and she realized that that, too, should have been put on to boil twenty minutes ago.

Cold pie?

'Chips,' she thought, suddenly. Mom always seemed able to produce platefuls of crisp golden chips at ten minutes' notice. 'Egg and chips. I'll cook my Friday Pie for supper.'

It was a good idea. The only trouble was that Ruth did not know that crisp golden chips can only be produced in ten minutes if you have lots of smoking-hot fat and not too many, well-dried potato chips. Her potatoes were already peeled and standing in a pan of cold water and Ruth thought it would speed the cooking-time to pile the whole quantity straight in with the tepid fat, and heat both together.

Quarter of an hour later, just as she was beginning to realize how wrong she was, she heard Tony's voice approaching down the lane. Stonily she tipped the greyish congealing mass on to the compost heap at the bottom of the garden and set the cold pie on the table.

Nobody complained, not even Tony, who was too busy telling her how hard he had worked all morning to notice what he was eating. Auntie Mary's pie was very good anyhow, but it did look a little bare until Uncle Jack produced the loaf of bread and Pete offered tomatoes around. Ruth felt they might be excused for wondering what she could have found to do with herself all those hours, and murmured something about getting a proper meal ready for the evening as she knew they would want to get back to the field quickly now. She need not have worried; men and children seldom think constructively about what a woman actually does under the guise of housework.

'Well,' said Uncle Jack, pushing back his plate at the end of the meal, 'I reckon I'd better get back to finishing off them stakes.' Uncle Jack was not one of the talkers and planners. This was partly because working away with a road-building construction company most of the year set him apart from the mainstream of village activities, but also because he was by nature a silent, unassuming man. He liked best to find a solid straightforward job within his compass, the kind of job that was dull and out of the limelight and tended to be overlooked by everybody else. He had spent the morning doggedly driving in stakes to mark off the various parking areas to be allocated to stock-lorries and cars in the field adjoining the one where the main events were taking place. His brother-in-law, Sam Morgan the policeman, had shown him where the barriers should run, and been called away to join in some urgent consultation on the main field. Uncle Jack had gone steadily on with the job by himself and was preparing to go back and work at it until it was finished, all afternoon and all evening if need be. The gates for the rodeo he had been asked to help with were not there when he had first arrived on the field. They had finally turned up just before dinner-time and a group of youths

46

had decided to take charge of them during the afternoon. Pete had managed to associate himself with the group so he, too, was anxious to get back in case too many other boys had latched themselves on to this prestige job.

The rodeo was a new venture for the Show. The older men were dubious about the innovation, but the younger ones who had seen one or two in action at neighbouring, more ambitious Shows, had pressed eagerly for it to be included in this year's attractions. They had won the day, and now felt responsible for seeing that the equipment was properly fixed up. The oldest of the Tygwyn boys, Kevin, was generally acknowledged to be the expert, and took over the operation. All morning, as the equipment had not come, he had been driving the tractor slowly round the ring while Pete, and Kevin's brother Tom, had lifted straw bales off the back of the trailer behind, and the smaller boys, Gary and Jimmy and Fish, and Tony for a while, had rolled them into position round the ring for people to sit on. So Pete and Tom had been on hand when Kevin was making up his crew to set up the rodeo.

'What's so special about these rodeo things?' asked Ruth, after Pete had been explaining all this to her. 'I mean, how do all the other ponies and cows and things come into the ring?'

'They come in through a gap in the fence, like sensible creatures,' said Uncle Jack, drily.

'Yeah, but the rodeo ponies aren't broken in, you know, they're really wild, some of them, and ...' began Pete, but Tony interrupted him.

'You know what a *rodeo* is, silly,' he said. 'These cowboys come in on these big horses, all rearing and bucking and trying to get them off, and they roll their eyes and their nostrils get all big, and if they throw their rider, they stomp on him and trample him to death. It's real dangerous!'

Ruth looked at Tony in sceptical silence, and Uncle Jack gave her one of his slow grins.

'It don't sound quite like Llanwern, do it?' he said.

47

'Well,' said Pete, a little uncomfortably. He felt he was being mocked. 'It's the same idea, only the ponies are smaller – and I don't suppose anyone will get trampled to death.'

'Good,' said Ruth.

'Wanna bet?' asked Tony.

'Anyway, the ponies aren't broken in, and the boys don't have any saddle or bridle or anything, so it's quite difficult to stay on,' said Pete. 'They have this sort of pen, see, like you use for catching up bullocks and such; they drive the pony in one end, and it's narrow, so as he can't turn round in it. There's a boy standing on top, with his feet one each side, and when the pony is underneath him, he drops on top, and grabs the mane, and the other fellows open the gate in front – that's the one that leads into the ring – and out goes the pony. The rider has to see how long he can stay on, see.'

'How long do they manage to stay on for?' asked Ruth.

Pete looked a little sheepish. 'I don't know, really,' he admitted. 'I've never actually seen one. But that's what Kevin says happens,' he added defensively.

'But you're going to have a try, Pete, aren't you?' said Tony.

'I'll see,' said Pete cautiously.

'I bet you'll be terrific, I wish I could have a shot at it. Do you think they'll let me?'

'No,' said Ruth.

'No,' said Pete. 'They might not let me. I think you're meant to be fifteen.'

'You could say you're fifteen,' said Tony. 'You're fourteen, aren't you?'

'Just,' said Pete. His birthday had passed scarcely noticed a couple of days after the crash.

'Nobody would know,' said Tony. 'I think you look fifteen, easy.'

'*You* won't be in charge of the rodeo,' said Ruth. 'I don't think anyone would put you at fifteen for a moment,' she added to Pete.

48

'It depends who's in charge,' said Pete. 'I mean, this isn't like New York. Most people pretty well know how old you are. But if it's Kevin, I dare say he'll let me and Tom have a go. It's not like some of the boys from other villages who'll be there. He does know we can both ride.'

'Can you?' said Ruth.

'Of course he can,' said Tony.

'A bit,' Pete conceded. 'Not so good as Tom, though, because they've always got ponies there on the farm he can ride any time.'

Uncle Jack finished drying his hands on the towel behind the door. 'Well, I'm off,' he said. 'Why don't you come up with Pete and Tony, and then you can look in at the farm when you're passing? It's not much fun down here on your own all day.'

Ruth's eyes strayed to where the sugar basin sat secretively over the still-unwashed ketchup stain, and thought of her own and Tony's unmade beds upstairs.

'I will come up,' she said, anxious not to appear unsociable, 'but in a little while. There's a few things here I want to do.' Uncle Jack nodded, and went out.

Pete was putting the milk jug back in the fridge. 'Hey,' he said, 'that looks good. I thought you said you couldn't cook?' He brought out the raw Friday Pie and sniffed at it enquiringly.

'Well, you're going to want something for supper,' said Ruth. 'It's probably horrible.'

'I'll tell you that later,' said Pete. He looked at it uncertainly. 'Oughtn't you to cook it, though?'

'Of course,' said Ruth. 'But not yet. It won't take that long.'

'Mum usually cooks things she's made straightaway, and takes them out when they're done and then puts them back in to hot up just before the meal,' said Pete. 'I don't know why, but that's what she always does.'

'Oh, yes,' said Ruth. 'How stupid of me. Why didn't I think of that?'

'Because you are stupid, that's why,' remarked Tony.

'I only know because when Mum's up at Nana's when I come home from school she very often leaves me something cooked in the fridge and I just stick it in the oven to get hot. At least, that's what I'm supposed to do, but usually I'm too hungry to wait, so I just eat it as it is. Mum don't know that, though.'

Ruth had never ever come home and found her mother out at a meal-time. She realized how much more self-reliant Pete was than she. Although he was an only child and she was the oldest of three, and a girl at that, it was he who was practised in fending for himself. It was not that Auntie Mary could not be bothered with him, but much of her life centred around caring for her old parents and mentally-handicapped sister who all lived in a cottage a mile out of the village, and with his father away most of the time Pete was accustomed to being in the house on his own. Ruth could never remember being alone in their New York apartment. It would have seemed strange, but here she had rather enjoyed her morning to herself until her cooking disasters caught up on her.

'I'll put it in now and it can cook while I'm doing the other things,' said. 'Then I can come and join you after I've taken it out.'

'Better put the oven on first, then,' Pete commented casually and went to switch it on.

Ruth hesitated a moment. Should she tell him why the Friday Pie hadn't appeared for dinner? Tony was still hanging around, so she decided not to.

After the boys had gone and the washing-up was completed and everything put away – Ruth was determined not to have to do the job twice this time – she branched boldly into a new field of domesticity and washed the table-cloth. That took her a long time, too, because she proceeded largely by trial and error and kept on breaking off in the middle to make the beds or sweep the floor or seize on any other job that sprang to mind as being the sort of thing she ought to be doing – or merely to stand and brood anxiously in front of the unco-operative oven door, wondering how her precious handiwork was faring behind it.

At length the jobs were done, and the pie was done, too – and really not looking too bad, Ruth thought with modest pride, as she carried it into the larder.

Now that there was nothing further to prevent her from going to join the others up at the showground, it became apparent to Ruth that she did not really want to go. Uncle Jack and Pete would both be busy about their various jobs, Uncle Jack solitary in his secluded corner, Pete among a gang of youths. Tony would either be bored by now, and become a nuisance to her, or happy with his friends and not want her. The two Tygwyn daughters were a good deal older than she – the oldest was twenty, and at college, and the next one came between Kevin and Pete's friend Tom, and was about seventeen. The youngest in the family was Gary, who was ten, and had been playing with Tony in the go-cart the day she had first met the old man. She did not quite know how to attach herself to the girls at Tygwyn, although they were expecting her.

Ruth stood and gazed out of the kitchen window, putting off the moment of decision. Beyond the hedge that bounded the back garden she could see the line of alders following the course of the stream. Further off, a big bluff ran down from the moor, and behind it, she knew, although she could not see it, lay the green and ancient wood where the old man lived. How much easier it would be to stroll away out of the back door and along the course of the stream and take a quiet look at his ramshackle home once more. She did not think she would mind much whether he were there or not; it was somewhere of her own to go, a private world where nobody expected anything of her.

It would not do, she realized. The old man had chosen the private world a long time ago, and let society get on without him. There was no gap in the community for him, among the team busily setting the showground to rights. There was a place for Ruth, though, cutting sandwiches and looking after Tony and dishing up Friday Pie for supper, and she supposed she must go and fill it.

She left the kitchen and walked resolutely towards the front door, but just as she was about to open it there was a loud knock. Ruth opened the door so quickly that it immediately crossed her mind that the caller must think she was lonely enough to spend her day waiting for just such a visit, and she blushed crossly. It was Sylvia, the younger of the Tygwyn daughters.

'I was just coming up to you,' said Ruth quickly.

'Oh, good,' said Sylvia. She was a cheerful girl, plodding good-naturedly through an A-level course that was rather above her head, and something of a favourite with the sixth-form boys. 'Mum wanted some stuff from the shop for sandwiches, so she said to call and see if you were at home and would like to come up for tea.'

'If I can help . . .' Ruth began. 'Tony only gave me your message today,' she went on, 'and I was coming up, only I wanted to get the housework done first.'

Sylvia sniffed. 'Something smells good,' she said. 'Been busy cooking?'

'Only a pie ready to heat up for supper,' said Ruth. It probably smelt better than it looked, so she did not offer to show the pie to Sylvia. Anyhow, too much fuss about it would look as though she had never done any cooking before.

'I've got loads of stuff to pick up at the shop,' said Sylvia. 'So I'm glad I've got you to help carry it.'

They set off up the street together, Sylvia talking away about the day's incidents, from which Ruth deduced that a state of cheerful confusion reigned at Tygwyn.

'Kate was going to run down and fetch all this stuff in the van,' she remarked, as Mrs Burns at the shop checked down her list and stowed sliced loaves and tins of meat and cucumbers and a good deal more into a large cardboard box. Kate was her elder sister. 'But the van wouldn't start, and Kevin's up at the field busy with this famous rodeo, and Dad's taken the car into town to find the chap who won last year's Beef Challenge Trophy because he hasn't returned it, and some cousins have arrived for the day from Cardiff, and the house is full of people trying to help and they don't know where nothing is' (like me, thought Ruth) 'so I've had to walk down to cart all this up. Lucky I've got you.'

It was lucky. 'I've given you a box with hand-holds at each end,' said Mrs Burns, 'so as you can carry it between you. Watch the bottom don't fall out. It's a good strong one, so it shouldn't, but you want to keep an eye on it.'

Keeping an eye on the bottom of a large and fully-loaded box which you are carrying with another person is an impossible feat, and it fell out about fifty yards up the street. Sylvia found this very funny, and Ruth began to laugh with her. At last, still giggling intermittently, they began to retrieve the scattered articles, when the sight of one tin of luncheon meat still rolling gently down the hill, way past the shop and on towards Ruth's house, set them off again.

'I'll get it,' cried Sylvia, starting down after it.

'No, I will,' said Ruth, and a race developed, which Ruth won because Sylvia laughed too much.

By this time they were back at Ruth's gate. 'Why don't we borrow Uncle Jack's wheelbarrow, and take it in that?' she suggested.

'What, this poor little tin?' asked Sylvia.

'No, all of it. If we get another box from Mrs Burns, it'll probably happen the same.'

'Brains,' 'said Sylvia. 'Must be nice to have them. Will Mr Jenkins mind, do you think?'

It didn't seem likely, so Ruth fetched the barrow and they took it up the street and loaded it.

If one has a loaded wheelbarrow and two people, it is

actually much easier for each person to push the wheelbarrow in turn, but taking a handle each can be a lot more fun, in the same way that a three-legged race produces many more thrills and spills than a straight sprint.

By the time Sylvia and Ruth had reached Tygwyn lane, using a short cut across the fields, they had experienced plenty of both. At first Sylvia tended to court disaster just for the fun of it, but after the tomatoes and cucumbers began to show signs of wear and tear, and one of the sliced loaves burst out of its wrappings, they began to give their minds to perfecting their joint skill, and trundled their load expertly up to the kitchen door with a sense of shared achievement.

After that it was easy for Ruth to feel one of the family. There was plenty to do, and Sylvia, who was a sociable soul, took it for granted they should do everything together. When in due course Mrs Thomas sent them up to the field to tell any of the men who wanted a cup of tea to come in and get it, Ruth realized she had never given another thought to Tony. He did not seem to be anywhere about, but then all the smaller boys except Gary had disappeared home for their teas, and Gary thought Tony had probably gone with one of them.

'Pete, you haven't seen him around?' asked Ruth.

'No,' said Pete, vaguely. 'He was with the other kids a while back.' Pete and Tom had been joined by a small dark boy called Alan, who was Tom's cousin from Cardiff, and the three of them seemed very absorbed in their own affairs.

'You don't need to worry,' said Tom. 'The only time I worry about Gary is when he *is* here.' Tom, she thought, treated Gary as an equal, but she regarded Tony as a little boy. 'Anyway,' he went on, 'he'll turn up when he's hungry, but I expect he's having tea up at Fish's.'

'I'm famished, any rate,' said Gary. 'Let's get in quick before that lot eat up all the tea.' There was a group of young fellows who had been working with Kevin sauntering across the fields towards the farm with Sylvia in their midst, talking and joking.

'What about Uncle Jack?' said Ruth. 'Where is he? Shall I go and tell him to come up to the farm?'

'Is he here?' asked the dark boy, Alan, eagerly. 'Where? I'll go and tell him.'

'Why is he so keen to see him?' asked Ruth. 'Does he know him?'

'Yeah, well,' said Pete, 'it's a long story.' He looked as though he would like to have continued, but did not know how to.

'Pete's dad saved his life,' said Tom. 'Go on, Pete, tell, her.'

Ruth looked at Pete expectantly.

'When we were up in Scotland, it was,' he said.

'Just the other day, you mean? While we were staying here, before ...?'

'That's right. Alan turned up at this island where Dad's firm are building a road. They'd been setting some explosives, and Alan nearly got himself blown up.'

'What happened?'

'Oh, Dad got him out in time.'

'Oh, you're hopeless,' said Tom. 'There were these rocks, exploding up in all directions, and one of them knocked Alan unconscious, and Pete's dad, he just walked right in and carried him to safety. That's right, isn't it, Pete?'

'Just about.'

'Pete saw it all happen, didn't you, Pete? It must have been terrifically exciting. They could both have been killed, easy.'

Ruth looked across at Uncle Jack, in the next field, resting on the handle of his sledgehammer and listening to Alan.

'I can just imagine Uncle Jack doing that,' she said. Pete was making patterns in the soft turf with the heel of his boot and seemed not to hear.

'Nutty,' said Tom cheerfully, 'just like Pete. Runs in the family, see. You wait till you see Pete in the rodeo tomorrow.'

'I haven't said I'm going in for it yet,' said Pete.

'Of course you are,' said Tom. 'I am, so you must.'

'Oh, come off it. You've done a heck of a lot more riding than me.'

'That's got nothing to do with it. This isn't proper riding. It's just a bit of fun.'

'You're not scared, are you, Pete?' asked Gary. 'Come on, let's go for tea. I'm famished.' He took Ruth's hand and they all started to run.

'What was Alan doing up in Scotland anyway?' panted Ruth.

'What was Pete doing, that's more to the point,' Tom replied, grinning.

Ruth decided it was not the right moment to pursue the subject, and anyway just then Alan caught up with them in the yard.

Kate was helping her mother look after the men, and Sylvia was surrounded by her own party of hungry youths, so the boys adopted Ruth as their personal waitress. When it was discovered that Sylvia had dispensed all the ham sandwiches to her friends, Tom and Alan prevailed on Ruth to make them some more.

'But I'm no good at cutting bread,' she objected, doubtful about helping herself in someone else's kitchen.

'There's a sliced loaf there,' said Tom. 'Looks as though it's been dropped in the mud. That'll do us.'

'It's for refreshments tomorrow.'

'Go on; you've got to feed us after we've been working all day. We'll be dead by tomorrow if you don't give us something to eat now.'

Indeed the whole place seemed to be bursting at the seams with food and, as Alan said, Ruth couldn't let the workers starve in the midst of plenty.

'Open another of those tins on the dresser,' said Sylvia, when Ruth asked her about more ham. 'Cheeky!' she added, as one of her clients lifted the lid of the teapot and peered in.

'Just wondering what you used for tea-leaves,' remarked the culprit, surveying a somewhat pale cup of tea.

'You shouldn't drink so much,' said Sylvia. 'Do those boys want any more tea down your way, Ruth?'

'Let me squeeze it for you,' offered another lad holding out a pair of brawny arms.

'Oh, I'll make another pot,' said Sylvia patiently. 'Give me that cup, Bill; I'll throw it out and you can have another from the fresh lot. I don't know where they put it all,' she added, coming over with the teapot to where Ruth was spreading butter, much too meticulously to please the boys.

'Come on, Ruth,' said Tom. 'Just slosh it on.'

'I'm next,' said Alan.

'I thought I was,' said Pete.

'When am I going to get mine?' asked Gary.

Under this sort of continuous pressure Ruth spread faster and faster, and by the time the boys were satisfied she was swirling the butter across and slapping on the slices of ham in fine style.

Then the men and boys drifted off, Uncle Jack back to his stakes and Kevin back to the collecting-ring for the rodeo, but Pete and Tom and Alan and Gary took their bicycles to practise for the bicycle race next day. Sylvia put the washing-up bowl in the sink and filled it deep with hot water, plunging in plump and capable arms and turning out the clean crockery at a great rate. Ruth helped Mrs Thomas with the drying-up while Kate kept bringing more loads of cups and saucers left by the men all over the house.

It was warm and companionable in the Tygwyn kitchen, and Ruth was as unwilling to leave as she had been to come. It was only when Mrs Thomas suggested they take the long white table-cloths up to the refreshment tent that evening and spread them out on the trestles the men had put up there, so that they should be ready for the first helpers to arrive in the morning, that she thought about Tony again.

'I expect you'll find him up there,' said Sylvia. 'They'll all be finishing up now, I expect, and packing it in for the night.'

Ruth had also remembered her pie. 'Anyway, I'll have to go home after we've put out the cloths and see to their supper,' she said. 'I'll take Tony back down with me.'

But Tony was still nowhere to be seen. All the other boys were playing around the end of the field set aside for sports, some on bicycles, some linked together in practice for a three-legged race, and others for the wheelbarrow. It reminded Sylvia of something.

'You mustn't forget to take back your uncle's wheelbarrow,' she said suddenly, watching them.

None of the boys could remember seeing Tony since before tea. Fish said they thought he had gone in to tea with Gary.

'No,' said Jimmy, 'he run off before that, because he couldn't join in our game.' He glanced at Ruth apologetically. 'I mean, he had been with Pete and them, and we was in the middle of something when he came, and we said he could join in the next one when we had finished, and he run off. Remember?'

'That's right,' said Gary. 'I forgot. Anyway, I thought he was still sticking around somewhere.'

'I thought he went back to Pete,' said Jimmy.

'No,' said Pete, when Ruth asked him. 'He didn't come back. Actually, I think he was a bit fed up with us, because we was busy, and he kept getting in the way, and somebody told him to shove off.' Pete, too, gave Ruth an apologetic look. 'It wasn't said nastily, just like one says it to any kid, but you know what Tony is.' He looked around the field, thinking. 'He may have gone over to see Dad,' he added. 'We can ask him now.'

Mr Jenkins was walking back across the field, his sledge-hammer over his shoulder and his solitary day's work done. 'Yeah,' he said. 'He came over to me one time, before tea that was. Wanted a job, he said, so I asked him if he could loop the twine across between the posts. He done it for a bit, but I think he must have found it a bit dull, because next time I looked he'd gone. I supposed he'd gone back to join the boys. I reckoned he must have had a bit of a tiff with some of them, and after he'd been along of me for a while he'd thought he'd best forget it if he didn't want to miss the fun.'

There weren't many people left on the field now, and those that Ruth asked could not remembering seeing Tony around since before tea.

'He'll have gone home, sure to,' they said. 'You'll find him waiting for you when you get back.'

They were quite right. When Ruth neared home, trundling Uncle Jack's wheelbarrow down the village street, with Uncle Jack beside her carrying his sledgehammer, there was Tony swinging on the gate.

'Hi,' he said, cheerfully enough. 'Where on earth have you been all this time?'

'Looking for you,' said Ruth swiftly, though it wasn't exactly true.

'What for?' said Tony. 'Did you think I'd get lost?'

'Well, no,' said Ruth. What she had thought was that he would be in such a temper because no one had been running after him that he would be impossible to live with all evening. 'But you weren't with the other boys, and so naturally I wondered what you were doing with yourself.'

Uncle Jack said, 'I'll take the barrow round the back.' He swung the sledgehammer off his shoulder, laid it carefully in the barrow and wheeled it round the side of the house. Tony watched him go.

'I was okay,' he said. 'I was with a friend.'

'Who?'

'He said he knew you. He took me to see some baby hedgehogs.' Tony looked up, smiling, suddenly excited and attractive. 'They were great. He said you'd seen them. Didn't you think they were great?'

'Yes,' said Ruth, 'but ...' She felt suddenly resentful. The hedgehogs were *her* secret. Maybe she would have told Tony about them in a day or two, and taken him to see them. But

59

the old man had no business to bring Tony into it without consulting her.

'But what?' asked Tony. He seldom spoke to her in that friendly, open way, but Ruth was not to be mollified.

'You know perfectly well you shouldn't go off like that with a strange man,' she said.

'You did,' said Tony, not unreasonably. 'And anyway, he's not a stranger. I've seen him around a lot. The boys call him Old Mossy.'

Chapter 4

'LOOK,' said Ruth to Tony after breakfast next morning, 'you're not to go chasing off after that man again today.'

'What man?' said Tony, though he knew perfectly well. He was sitting on the floor of his bedroom tying the laces of his baseball boots while Ruth was making his bed. 'I wish you'd smooth the bottom sheet properly like Mom does. I can't get to sleep when it's all lumpy like that.'

'Fusspot,' said Ruth. 'You should learn to make your bed yourself. You know who I mean – the hedgehog man.'

'Old Mossy? Well, you did.'

'I'm older. Anyway, I just happened to come upon his hut in the woods when I was out for a walk. I didn't go off with him.'

'Well, he's okay, isn't he? I liked him. He listens, instead of just bla-bla-ing all the time like most grown-ups.'

'Yes,' said Ruth. 'But I don't think Mom would like it if she knew you'd gone wandering off with him yesterday like that.'

'You needn't tell her,' said Tony.

'There's Uncle Jack.'

'He wouldn't mind.'

'No, but you can't ask him not to mention it to Auntie Mary or Mom. You can't ask grown-ups not to tell each other things, even Uncle Jack,' said Ruth.

'As a matter of fact,' said Tony consideringly, 'I don't think Uncle Jack was there when I said yesterday about going to see Old Mossy.'

Ruth said nothing, but Tony sensed she had taken his point.

61

'Anyhow,' Tony went on, 'it's okay. The boys do know him, truly. He shoots rabbits at Tygwyn and at the Rhos and that; I was playing with Jimmy up at the Rhos one day and I saw Mr Price – you know, Jimmy's mother – I saw her give him a sack of potatoes. She called him by his Christian name – Bert or something, I forget, but that means she must know him pretty well, doesn't it?'

'Well, okay,' said Ruth. 'But don't go buzzing off with him up to that wood today.' It was funny how she had already come round to thinking of Old Mossy as Tony's person, although it was she who had discovered him first.

'Course not,' said Tony. 'It's the Show, isn't it? I don't want to miss that.'

'And I promised Mrs Thomas Tygwyn I'd help at the refreshment tent this morning,' said Ruth, 'so you'll know where to find me. Will you be okay joining up with the other boys?'

'I guess so,' said Tony, avoiding her glance. If he had not met up with Old Mossy and spent an exciting afternoon with him, he would have run to Ruth full of indignation about the village boys not wanting to play with him. As things were, though, he decided it would be better to say nothing about it. He did not know what the other boys had told Ruth when she was looking for him after tea yesterday, but he had a feeling she might not be a sympathetic audience. Anyhow, yesterday was yesterday.

'I'll give you your entrance money, then,' said Ruth. 'Auntie Mary left some for the Show. You can come to the refreshment tent to get your lunch, can't you? That's what Pete and Uncle Jack will do.'

'There'll be an ice-cream truck,' said Tony, watching Ruth checking through the change. 'And a stand with crisps and candy and that. And there's guessing the weight of a ram, and what they call a skittle alley, and children's races, and clay-pigeon shooting . . .'

'That's for the men,' said Ruth firmly. 'I'll give you twenty-five pence now, and if you need any more you can come find me.'

Ruth was looking forward to helping in the refreshment tent. She had enjoyed her busy afternoon up at Tygwyn the day before, when there had been plenty for her to do, and in the cosy friendly atmosphere of the farm she had found herself able to cope quite well with the sandwich-cutting and the tea-making and the dishes, and nobody had stood around expecting her to make conversation. Then, after the slight anxiety about missing Tony, it was a relief to find him at home and in a good mood, and even the Friday Pie had turned out a success at supper. The morning had broken with a slight mist in the air, a touch of early autumn, and Uncle Jack had forecast a sunny day. All in all, it promised to be a good day. Ruth became aware that the feeling that shafted through her like the sun's rays through the thinning mist was, quite simply, happiness.

'Come on,' she said, running her hand over Tony's hair in an unaccustomed gesture, 'let's walk up to the field together.'

Tony ducked away, but did not really mind. He grabbed her by the hand and raced with her down the stairs.

They cut across the field behind the house, Tony talking most of the way about Old Mossy's home in the woods, but after awhile he fell silent and seemed to be thinking. Just before they got to the Tygwyn gate, he said suddenly, 'I do *wish* they would let me see Patsy.'

It was the first time since the accident that Ruth had got so far into the morning without actually thinking about Patsy.

'Patsy?' she said, momentarily surprised. 'Well, never mind, you'll be seeing her quite soon when she comes out of hospital.' She waved at Sylvia, who was coming out of the house with a couple of massive enamel teapots. 'Hang on a minute,' she called. 'I'll take one of those, shall I?'

'I want to see her now,' said Tony. 'Tomorrow, anyway.'

'Well, you can't,' said Ruth. 'I've told you over and over, the hospital won't allow young children to visit. Look, there's

Gary. Do you want to go see him?' She hurried off to join Sylvia.

Up at the showground, the main ring was deserted and though the area roped off by Uncle Jack the day before was filling up fast with stock-lorries there were few cars yet. The competition tents, however, were buzzing with activity, as exhibitors struggled to beat the deadline when the judges would move in with their little notebooks and the red, blue and green cards to denote first, second and third prizes.

They looked in at the horticultural tent, where Uncle Sam, with slow deliberate hands, was setting out three massive onions, each one gilded and symmetrical as the dome of a mosque.

In the next tent, labelled 'Handicrafts', lace-edged table-cloths jostled with stuffed knitted giraffes and quilted cushion covers, and a fierce female steward was trying to expel the gossiping exhibitors. The other competition sections were all for children, and these were assembled in a three-sided marquee. Small boys strolled casually in and deposited dog-eared bits of paper bearing spirited scenes of the hay harvest or Perseus slaying the Gorgon; older girls laid out babies' layettes or hand-sewn aprons with all the window-dressing panache they could muster.

'When did Tony do that?' said Ruth, seeing his name on one of the pictures. 'He didn't say he was entering for it.'

'Oh, he did that up at our place one night,' said Sylvia. 'Gary was doing one, so the two of them decided to go in for it.' Both pictures showed a tractor pulling a trailer loaded with bales to an impossible height and surrounded by dogs and boys.

'I don't think much of Tony's handwriting,' said Ruth, but privately she thought his drawing was better than Gary's. She was surprised that he had not told her he had entered the competition, or boasted about his chance of winning.

There were two busy women up at the refreshment tent lighting the calor gas boiler and dusting out the cups and saucers before setting them in battalions along the trestle tables, but nobody else was yet about so the girls wandered off for a longer look around.

A knot of youths was standing a few yards away from the sheep-pens, where two small, wrinkled men wearing judges' badges studied the prisoners. The ewes huddled together, heads down, their flanks heaving and steaming lightly in the cool morning air, puzzled as children on their first day at school, shy rather than frightened. Further along, the rams put a bolder face on life, each alone in his pen, yellow eyes staring out of an obtuse face with its bony Roman nose. Tom rode by on a shaggy pony, leading two others.

'They for the rodeo, Tom?' asked Sylvia.

'That's right.'

'Not Shandy, surely?' Shandy was the pony Tom was riding.

'Not unless they're short.'

'Oh, Tom, Shandy would never buck anyone off.'

'I thought rodeo ponies had to be wild, never ridden before,' said Ruth. Quite apart from Shandy, who was an old family pet, the other two ponies looked remarkably docile.

Tom looked a little embarrassed. 'Yeah, well,' he said, 'like I said, Shandy's not going in the ring unless he has to. These two aren't broken in, truly. Well, not really.'

Ruth put her hand out to stroke one of them. It rolled a nervous eye at her and jerked its head uneasily, then lowered its head and tore at the grass as though it hadn't eaten for a month. It did not look like one of Tony's cowboy-killers.

'There aren't all that number of ponies around that aren't broken in at all,' said Tom. 'But remember you've got to jump on and hang on without any saddle or bridle or anything; it's not that easy, when they're all excited by the crowd and the noise and some other fellow gives it a whack behind just as you get on.' He trotted off with his charges to a small fenced-off area at the end of the field where already a number of modest-looking ponies were peacefully grazing. Soon afterwards a stock-lorry lurched past the girls and they could see between the slats the round rumps and wide startled eyes of quite a number of ponies. The driver turned and backed his lorry right up to the makeshift gate into the enclosure, shouting to Tom, who had just released his ponies, to open back the wire-netting for him.

Pete appeared from somewhere, with Gary and Tony, and while they held the ends of the fence against the side of the lorry the driver came and let down the tailboard. At first no animal appeared, but then he banged on the side with the flat of his hand, and a whole bevy of excited little rough hill ponies came skidding and whickering down the ramp. Their arrival caused quite a commotion among the other horses, and for a while there was enough bucking and stampeding and even a few flurried kicks to impress Tony with the genuine wildness of the creatures.

'Which one are you going to ride, Pete?' he asked.

'None probably,' said Pete. 'I told you, I'm not old enough.'

'Oh, go on, Pete,' said Tom. 'Nobody's going to ask how old you are. I'm going to have a bash, anyhow.'

'I'll see,' said Pete nonchalantly.

'You needn't worry they won't let you,' said Tom. 'Kevin said he wouldn't stop me having a go, and if he lets me go, then he must let you.'

'Pity,' said Pete, grinning. He wants Tom to think he's joking, thought Ruth, but he isn't, not really. He wants not to be allowed to clamber on to one of those rough wild-eyed little ponies and be hurled out into the middle of the ring watched by a crowd of people, to be flung ignominiously and perhaps painfully on to the sun-baked field, to roll clear from those sturdy prancing hoofs and make the long trek back to the ring-side on his own unsteady feet. It surprised her that she should know that Pete was scared and Tom should not, because she always thought of Pete as being much closer to Tom than he was to her. After all, they had grown up together and gone to the same school all their lives.

'What about you?' Pete asked Alan, who had just joined them. 'Are you risking your neck in the rodeo?'

'Not likely,' said Alan, cheerfully. 'I'm only a poor city boy; I don't know one end of a horse from the other. I'll get all the fun I want watching you fellows.'

Now is the moment, thought Ruth, for Pete to come out boldly with Alan and say he doesn't want to have a go either, but Pete said nothing. To help him, she said, lightly, 'If I were you, Pete, I wouldn't go, either,' but Pete just said, 'Well, you're not,' rather shortly, and walked away.

Sylvia had joined the group of youths watching the sheep classes being judged, but now she called across to Ruth to say she could see people beginning to go into the refreshment tent and she thought they had better go and see if help was needed. The next two hours passed quickly, as Ruth dispensed sandwiches and struggled with the unfamiliar British change. There was plenty to do and Ruth, though thoroughly enjoying the bustle, was beginning to wilt, when Tony arrived, brandishing treasure. 'Hi, Ruth, look what I've got.'

'What? ... That'll be twenty-seven pence. Twenty-eight, twenty-nine, thirty. That's right, isn't it? Where did you get those from, Tony? What are they, anyway?'

'They're clays. What can I have to eat? I'm famished. Can I just take a plate and choose?'

'Three cups of tea – did you say two with sugar? – six sandwiches and a packet of biscuits ... that'll be ... yes, that's right, thank you.'

'Can you keep them for me, Ruth? I can't carry them around.'

'What are they? Look, can't you see I'm busy? What am I meant to do with them?'

'They're the clay pigeons. I told you. I need somewhere safe to put them. And I want something to eat.'

Ruth was mystified. 'Where did you get them?' she asked suspiciously. 'They don't look like pigeons to me.' In fact they looked like ribbed black saucers with yellow circles on them; Tony appeared to be clutching about half-a-dozen.

'Put them under the table, Tony,' said Sylvia. 'There's a fresh pot coming now, Mrs Moss, if you can wait a minute. They should be safe enough there.'

'They break easily,' said Tony, handing them over to Ruth. 'Don't drop them whatever you do.'

'But what are they *for*?'

'Oh I dunno. But all the boys collect them. Gary must have hundreds. The man lets off this great sort of catapult, okay? And this saucer goes whizzing through the air and the guy fires at it, and if he hits it he scores, and if he misses, it very often drops to the ground without breaking, and us kids rush forward between whiles and see how many we can pick up. It's great. I'm going back there after to pick up some more.'

'But what do you *do* with them?' asked Ruth. There was a bit of a lull, and she was counting out some money for Tony's sandwiches.

'I'm going to keep them,' said Tony. 'They're neat.' His nose was faintly beaded with sweat, his shirt hanging out behind, and the pride of ownership swelled in him like a bubble.

'They all do,' said Sylvia, 'Tom used to, and Kevin. I remember Kevin having a great pile in the farmyard, and I got in among them and bust them. He was mad at me – I was only about five, I suppose. It's like conkers, and dead fireworks after Bonfire night. It's just one of those things.'

She spoke in the tones of amused affection she habitually used when commenting on the opposite sex.

'But don't they mind?' said Ruth. She felt as though she were being asked to harbour stolen goods.

'I think they're meant to hand in the unbroken ones,' said Sylvia, 'but nobody bothers much. The boys get a lot of fun out of it.'

Ruth said no more. She had assumed until then that in clay-pigeon shooting the competitors really shot at actual clay pigeons. She had heard the bang, bang, of the guns at regular intervals all morning in the adjacent field and when, in answer to her question, Sylvia had said it was the clay-pigeon shooting competition she had felt quite worried at the apparent destruction of so many expensive model birds.

'Come see for yourself, after,' Tony begged her. 'It's really great.'

'I'm rather busy,' said Ruth, somewhat pleased with the fact, but by now the main rush was easing off, and the helpers were beginning to stand about and gossip between carrying loads of crockery to the washers-up at the back of the tent.

'You go along,' said Mrs Thomas. 'Only have something to eat yourselves first. You don't want to spend all day stuck in this old tent.'

Ruth was not sure about that. The refreshment tent was a secure anchorage. However, Sylvia expressed her intention of seeing how her various friends among the young farmers had got on in the stock-judging classes, and Tony was unexpectedly eager to share his fun with Ruth, so after they had both filled themselves stodgily full of sandwiches they set off together for the clay-pigeon shooting field.

That was when the gilt of the day began to wear thin for Tony. They met Gary and his friends coming away from the clay-pigeon shoot, arms full of trophies. Ruth could see they had more than Tony.

'Where are you going?' said Tony. 'I'm just coming back.'

'It'll be the Grand Parade soon,' said Gary, 'and the children's sports after, and then the rodeo, so we're going to get something to eat.'

'Hey, that kid's got a Supertoff,' said Jimmy, pointing to a child licking a gaudy ice-cream. 'Let's go to the ice-cream van on the way.' They all moved off towards the van with its cluster of clients.

Tony hovered, undecided. 'Shall we go get them now, before the clay pigeons? I have the ice-cream money you gave me.'

'Do you still want to go over there?' asked Ruth. 'Wouldn't you rather go back to the ring with the boys?'

It was a difficult decision. In his mind's eye Tony could see the armful of clays Gary had been carrying; he could also see the gang of boys chatting and laughing in the ice-cream queue. 'Come on,' he said. 'Maybe I could pick up a whole bunch now the other kids have gone.'

It was a vain hope. Another group of boys from a different village had taken up the best vantage point, and though they waited about for fifteen minutes Tony was only able to collect one broken clay. Then there was a pause in the shooting. The other boys went away, but Tony kept Ruth hanging on.

'I'm the only one after them now,' he said hopefully. 'They'll be starting again in a minute.'

He was wrong, though. After a further wait, it became clear that the shooting had packed up. Tony went up to the man at the catapult.

'When are you starting again?' he asked.

'Not till after the judging in the main ring is over,' the man answered. 'The shooting makes the horses nervous.'

'Let's get those ice-creams,' said Ruth quickly. 'Then we can go find the others at the main ring.'

They joined a long queue at the ice-cream van and it was some time before they neared the front. At that point, the man said something to the two boys next in line, and pulled down the shutter.

'What's he done that for?' said Tony.

'Sold out,' said the boy in front. 'Just our luck. Come on, Phil, let's see what they've got up at the refreshment stall.'

Tony was less philosophical. This was the second fist to be smashed through the window of his perfect day.

'It's not fair,' he shouted, stamping and scowling at Ruth.

'I'm sorry, Tony, I really am,' said Ruth.

'It's all your fault, anyway,' said Tony, the angry flush spreading up to his fair hair. 'You should have let me go first.'

Ruth knew Tony too well to think this worth contradicting, but her sympathy began to ebb.

Her silence must have made its point, though, for Tony began to cast around for other scapegoats. 'It's those other boys, greedy pigs, getting in first. I bet they hogged two apiece, Gary and them. I hate them!'

Knots of people gossiping near by began to look around, part sympathetic, part disapproving, for Tony's flat American tones, boosted by fury, carried a long way.

'Oh, shut up, Tony,' said Ruth. 'You know perfectly well it's nobody's fault, it's just one of those things, so you can stop making an exhibition of yourself.'

Tony glared at her a moment, then his face sagged and his eyes grew wet. 'I want . . .' he began, and stopped.

'. . . Mommy!' said Ruth. The mockery in her voice took them both aback. For a moment she felt ashamed, wanted to unsay it, wanted to hug him, to buy him a hundred ice-creams, give him the moon. But he just stood there, the hard look spreading back over his face as he muttered, 'Well, you're no good, that's for sure.'

The compassion ebbed in Ruth as quickly as it had flowed, and left a gritty tidemark of revenge – revenge for the people standing near by laughing at them, revenge for the slights he had heaped on her in the weeks of her despair, revenge because he wanted her mother, her aunt, her sister, everyone but her. She had it in her power to hurt him, and hurt him she would.

'Well, you haven't got Mommy,' she said, 'so you can't run to her. And you haven't got Auntie Mary, either, so you can't run to her. And you haven't got Patsy, and you can't run to her because the hospital won't let her be bothered by such a stupid little baby as you.' She thought of saying, 'And you can't run to Daddy,' but knew, because he was dead, she must not say that, so the need in her to strike and go on striking sought for other outlets. 'Of course,' she said, more slowly, more cunningly, 'you can run to Pete if you like, or Gary.' For she knew that Pete had grown tired of Tony since Alan came, and Gary and his mates had grown tired of Tony time and again whenever the childish mood came over him, and she knew that Tony knew that, too.

So you've got no one but me, she thought, but she did not say so because there was no need. As she looked at Tony's face, expressionless now, she just did not know whether, boylike, he had shut his ears to the words and his face was blank because his mind was blank, or whether the blank look was a cloak for a desperate hurt. As she wondered, she knew that her words had outrun her anger. How difficult it was to make words match the inner mind. Either they churned about unspoken in a bottleneck while emotion boiled below, unguessed at, or came streaming out frothing the matter to twice its proper size, like lemonade poured into a glass from a height.

She was not contrite, yet, but she knew she had over-reached the mark, and looked about for something to say or do that would balance things out.

'Come on,' she said. 'Let's go see the big parade or whatever they call it. You and I must be the only people here who don't know what it's all about.'

She watched Tony narrowly to see if he was going to cry, or rage, or bounce back, but he was still looking as though he weren't listening.

'Maybe they'll get in some more ice-cream later and open up the truck again.' She paused. 'I could go bang on the window and ask, I guess. Or you could.'

'You ask, if you want. I don't care. I'd rather spend my money on something else,' said Tony. He sounded merely bored. He started to walk off towards the ring, not running away, just walking, as though he had been passing the time of day with an acquaintance and now they were each going about their business.

Ruth followed him uneasily. 'Shall I go put that clay with the others for you?' she suggested.

Tony looked at the object in his hand – as though he had forgotten about it. 'I don't want it. It's broken.' He flung it into the hedge.

'Litter lout,' said Ruth, before she could stop herself.

'Go pick it up, then,' said Tony, and walked unconcernedly off.

Ruth wandered around outside the ring of people until she heard her name being called, and there were Alan and Tom and Pete, beckoning her to come over and join them. It was an unexpectedly friendly gesture, because though she and Pete got on quite happily together at Pete's home she did not expect to share in his life with his friends. She suspected it was Alan who had called her; he was more spontaneously sociable than the country boys. He was a good person to have around on an occasion like this. Bland in his urban ignorance – rather proud of it, in fact – he asked the most basic questions and passed the most absurd comments on all the animals that lumbered and pranced before them, and Tom, who took his farming seriously, did his best to answer them.

Pete was silent, as though he had something on his mind, but he cheered up when it was announced that the sports would be starting at the other end of the field. They all moved off in that direction, and Ruth was relieved to see that Tony had joined up with Fish, and was practising for the three-legged race with him. They were not a great success at it. In the event, they came rather spectacularly last, and Ruth could see them, hobbling off the field heaping recriminations on each other while still incongruously yoked together at the ankle. She forebore to interfere and merely noted with relief that Tony appeared to be himself again.

Tom and Pete both entered for the one-mile race, which was mainly the preserve of lads in their late teens. Alan declined; Ruth noticed he was choosy about what he would go in for, only selecting events where he had a good chance of winning, and always did – not, she thought, that she could blame him, as she herself had no intention of going in for anything at all. Tom and Pete, on the other hand, put themselves down for everything, as did most of the local boys. 'It doesn't cost anything to enter,' said Pete, 'so you've got nothing to lose.'

'Nothing to gain, either,' said Tom, ruefully, who had not managed to get placed in any event, but was not deterred from trying again.

'Gluttons for punishment,' said Alan, and Tom readily agreed.

'I suppose it's living in the country,' said Alan to Ruth, as Tom and Pete went off to join the boys at the start of the one-mile course. They sat on the ground and watched the circling runners.

'Hullo,' said Alan after a while, 'Tom's had enough.' The runners were veering round the bend at the end of the second lap, and Tom, well at the back, pulled straight ahead and flopped on the grass beside them.

'Hey, Tom,' said Alan, 'there's another two laps to run yet. Hadn't you better get back out on that track?'

'You'll be lucky,' panted Tom. 'How's Pete doing?' he added after he had got some of his breath back, rolling over and propping himself up on his elbows to see.

'Still running,' said Ruth. 'But rather far behind. All the other boys are much bigger,' she added defensively.

'Oh, Pete won't give up,' said Tom. 'I bet some of the other blokes will, though. Look, I told you.' The two boys immediately in front of Pete had pulled out, and another one nearer the front dropped to a walk. Two others were fading fast, and Pete, jogging steadily on, overtook them at the beginning of the last lap.

'Good old Pete,' said Tom, and Alan yelled, 'Come on, Pete! Keep it up!' Ruth said nothing, but she found she was clenching her hands tight. This race seemed different from

74

the others, more serious, more heroic. Pete, struggling doggedly over the tussocky grass in pursuit of those four long-legged young men, seemed to epitomize everything that was worth while about life. 'Please,' she cried out in the silence of her mind, 'please, I know he can't win, it doesn't matter about beating the others, but please, don't let him not finish, please, let him finish well.'

Unexpectedly one of the leaders stumbled and took himself out of the race; he was a favourite from previous years and did not fancy being an also-ran. Pete came in third out of the four finishers.

Ruth glanced around to see if other onlookers besides themselves had recognized Pete's achievement, but there were very few about, for most people were still around the main ring. Not even Tony had stayed to witness Pete's epic struggle.

The rodeo would be a different matter. That was scheduled to take place in the main ring immediately the parade was over, and Ruth had heard a good many references to it among the people at the Show already that day. There was no doubt it was going to be a star attraction.

Already a group of youths were helping Kevin re-align the fencing to make a corridor from the collecting-ring, where the shaggy little wild ponies were grazing, into the main ring, through the steel cattle-pen that was being used as a gate. They realized that the announcer was calling for competitors to gather by the entrance and to give in their names to Kevin Thomas, and casual groups of boys, and some laughing girls in old jeans, were making their way across.

'Come on,' said Tom to Pete. 'Let's get over there.'

'I'm not going till near the end. I've got to get my breath back,' said Pete.

'More fool you to have run all the way,' said Tom. 'You should have stopped halfway, like me, and kept your breath for the big time.'

Ruth was resentful. She knew Tom had not really dropped

out deliberately, but she guessed he had not cared particularly about the race because his interest centred on the rodeo. It was unfair that he should go out there in front of all those packed crowds around the ring and excel over Pete, who had fought his battle unsung.

Tom and Alan were going on ahead, and Pete followed a short distance behind.

'Pete,' she said, 'you were awfully good in that mile; I didn't know you could run so well.'

'I get quite a lot of practice at school,' said Pete. He looked at her, a little pink and surprised that she should have cared enough to come out with it. 'Anyway, I wasn't that good. I wasn't even placed.'

'No, but you beat lots of boys who were much older than you. You could easily have given up, like Tom.'

'Oh, Tom isn't really a runner. He only came in for a bit of a lark. Riding's his thing, you'll see.' He spoke with such unaffected pride that Ruth warmed to him.

'I don't see why you have to go in for the rodeo if you don't want to,' she said. 'Alan isn't.'

There was a pause before Pete replied: 'I never said I didn't want to' – long enough for Ruth to know he really didn't. He heard the pause, too, and added quickly, 'There's nothing to worry about. I've fallen off ponies often in the past. It's only a bit of fun.' As he moved off after Tom, Ruth could hear Tom shouting over the mob of boys around Kevin, 'Put me and Pete down, Kevin, won't you?' and saw Kevin glancing in Pete's direction and nodding as he added names to his list.

Alan grabbed her, saying, 'Let's get in here,' and steered Ruth up to the ropes just by the gate, so that they were between the spectators on their one side and the boys waiting to have their turns on the other. Tom and Pete edged in close by them.

Ruth noticed a strapping lad standing astride the side bars of the pen, and thought at first he was merely adjusting it, but

76

then suddenly with a lot of whooping and shouting an excited and scared little pony came tearing down the corridor. Somebody grabbed it as it was brought up short by the gate, the boy above dropped down on its back, the gate was opened, and they were out in the ring. The boy had one hand twisted in the mane and he leant well back, his long legs stiff out in front of him, almost under the pony's chin. Small though the animal was, it had thick sturdy legs and stamped them on to the hard soil like pile-drivers, the front two together, then the back, and sometimes all four at once. With every jar, the boy jolted further and further sideways until he was hanging almost head downwards, and finally he fell, awkwardly, on his shoulder, one arm bent backwards, and it seemed impossible that the plunging hoofs should miss him.

They did, though, and the pony charged away half across the field as though the devil were after it, and then, as suddenly as it had started, it stopped, and coolly began to graze, way out in the middle of the ring. The youth picked himself up, grinning for all the world to see it was a good joke, and not think a sore arm was anything for a young farmer to make a fuss about. Tom laughed loudly, and so, after a moment, did Pete; in fact, all the waiting competitors made a great show of amusement. The mere spectators could afford to look sympathetic, or even frightened when the plunging horses came close to the ropes.

The young man made his way to the exit, and another boy mounted the bars. This time it was quite a large horse that came running down the corridor; when the gate was opened it ran straight on out into the ring, not bucking once, and the rider had an easy time of it until, right in the middle, the horse reared up without warning, and the boy rolled straight off backwards, without any fight at all.

Boy followed boy on ponies of every size and colour; some ponies were more obstreperous, or more scared, than others, and some boys stayed on longer than others, but for all of them the end was the same – a riderless pony grazing at the far end of the ring, and for the rider a stiff smile on the long foot-journey home. There was also relief.

'You can laugh,' shouted one cheerful red-headed young giant as he rejoined his mates. 'You've got your turn coming.'

By halfway through only one rider had managed to stay aloft. Some of the lads were biting stubby nails, or rubbing tense hands up and down their jeans; there was a smell of sweat in the air, part nervous horse, part nervous boy. Each one wore his air of jocular unconcern like an old sack, in an attempt to hide the nervous animal wriggling inside. Ruth looked round for Pete, and found he was gone.

For a moment she thought he had slipped away altogether, and relief struggled with disappointment, but then she saw him. He was up aloft on the bars arguing with another boy below.

'You can just stew,' he was saying, with unusual petulance. 'I'm not coming down for anybody.'

'Kevin said I could go next, didn't you, Kev?'

Kevin was grappling with the next pony as it came charging down the passage. He sized up the arguing boys, and glanced at the raw-boned, wild-eyed creature which at present was trying to run backwards away from the gate.

'This one's for Glyn,' he acknowledged. 'Come off it, Pete, you can go next.' He turned and muttered to one of his helpers, 'Tell them to send up a small one next time.'

Pete clambered down, sulky because he had wound himself up for nothing, and Glyn got up, a big ungainly youth with broad hips and large hands. He stood across the rails, and dropped on the pony a second too soon, before it was right up to the gate. The pony stumbled, head down, just at the same instant as a helpful joker gave the animal a slap on the rump. The rider, taken unawares, slid straight off over the head of the pony into the small confined space between the animal and the still-unopened gate, and it seemed to Ruth that the pony

78

must surely trample him to death, as it reared and bucked, fenced closely in on every side.

The people on the further side of the main ring could not see what was happening, and continued to talk and laugh, but a fearful silence fell upon those around the gate, and when Kevin yelled, 'Open the gate, quick,' they could all hear the panic in his voice. This was no joke.

Somebody pulled up the gate and the pony bounded rider-less forward. The crowd murmured when they saw it, and then laughed as someone shouted, 'Missed his turn, has he?' Then Glyn unrolled from the ball he had flung himself into, and climbed to his feet.

'You all right?' asked Kevin.

'Yes, yes,' said Glyn, turning his head first on one side and then the other to shake the mud out of his ears. It was a joke, after all, and the boys began to jeer good-naturedly at him. But Ruth noticed that the back of the hand he had used to cover his face was grazed, and there was a jagged tear in his pullover, and under the mud his face looked blanched.

'Give him another turn,' shouted a well-meaning friend. 'You can't call that a proper turn.'

'Who said I wanted another turn?' countered Glyn.

'You can't go this time, anyhow,' said Kevin. 'She's not big enough for you. Up you get, then, Pete.'

A small palomino came cantering down to the pen; it was the same one Sylvia had ridden the first time round.

'I hope Kevin doesn't think he's going to palm me off with one of those midgets,' grumbled Tom. 'Poor old Pete; I'll bet he's cross.'

'I'll bet he isn't,' said Alan swiftly. His lean face was serious. 'I wouldn't want to go at all, not after what's just happened.'

'You didn't anyway,' said Tom. 'That was just a bit of bad luck. Anyway, Glyn wasn't hurt.'

'There he goes,' said Alan. Pete was astride the pony, nose

79

held firmly down by Kevin until the gate was opened, and then he was out in the ring.

Ruth wished she had seen him before he went, to wish him luck, but it was too late now; the circle of faces round the ring was nothing more than a blurred background for Pete in his private, lonely battle out there.

He did not do too badly, for the pony was a fairly easy ride. It bucked and reared enough to make a bit of a showing, but without a great deal of conviction.

'Pete wants to tug the mane harder,' said Tom. 'Some of the fellows come away with handfuls of the stuff. She isn't really trying to get him off.'

As though to give him the lie, the little palomino gave a spirited pirouette, followed by a shake and a sharp turn to the right, and Pete was deposited in a neat heap in the middle of the ring.

Tom muttered again that he hoped he would have a more lively ride, but Ruth felt like blessing the generous pony who had given Pete his test so sweetly, and tossed him so cleanly away from her own hard little hooves.

Pete came walking nonchalantly back towards them, one of the light-hearted crew whose ordeal was over. Standing beside them by the rope, he was full of chat now, telling Alan and Ruth things about the different ponies, and their various riders, and exchanging comments with the other youths who had completed their rides. Before, he had not spoken with the other competitors, except Tom, letting them think he was not one of them, only a small boy watching. Now he seemed taller and older, and held his head as high as any of them.

Tom felt it was time he, too, won his spurs, and he shouldered his way through to the pen.

'Good luck,' said Pete and Alan, but Ruth, although she smiled at him, said nothing. She felt it would be unfair, because she had missed the chance of saying it to Pete.

Meanwhile, Glyn was bravely mounting the pen once more.

This time, he entered the ring without mishap, and managed to cling to his perch until the final whistle.

So Tom awaited his mount knowing that two riders had kept on for the full time, and if he wanted to be in among the winners, so must he. The skinny black pony fell to his lot; it was long-legged and nervy, and scuttered down to the pen like a crab, sideways, tossing its head about.

'Rather him than me,' commented Pete.

'He doesn't look too bothered,' said Alan, for Tom was whistling absent-mindedly as he concentrated on the job.

'Tom's no more scared of a horse than you are of a football,' said Pete.

Tom was on the black pony now, but they were having some trouble getting it through the opening, because it reared up so high its head came above the lower bar of the gate. The lads all round tried to push it down, and it got one front hoof over the rail at the side.

'Get off on to the rails, Tom,' shouted Kevin. He did not distrust Tom's horsemanship, but the situation looked nastily as though it might develop into a repetition of what had happened to Glyn. But Tom just crouched low over the horse's neck, and as soon as it came down to earth again he coaxed it out into the ring. The pony continued to prance sideways in a series of uneven bolts. Tom swayed with the movement, looking perfectly balanced, as though he grew out of the animal's back. Teetering diagonally, the horse very soon came up against the rope, and the crowd surged nervously backwards. One broad farmer stood his ground, however, and clapped his hands resoundingly.

'Get away!' he shouted. 'Get away over!'

The horse got away. It rose up erect on startled hind-legs, till Tom's face was pressed against the pony's in an effort to keep in balance, then plunged down in a right-about-face and charged straight for the rope on the opposite side of the ring, where the crowd was thinnest. There was a sudden panic scattering and, seeing a gap miraculously appear in the wall of faces, the horse jumped clean out of the ring. It stopped a moment to take its bearings, reared a couple of times, then tore off again in the direction of the enclosure where the rodeo ponies were corralled. Mothers with pushchairs and children with ice-lollies scampered unceremoniously, and Ruth in a split-second diversion saw Tony and thought, he's got his ice-cream after all. Suddenly the pony realized that a stout fence separated him from his friends, and he skithered to a halt, all four stiff legs making muddy skid-marks in the grass. The horse stayed outside, but Tom sailed straight over the fence among the waiting ponies.

An ironic cheer went up as Tom climbed back out, quite unruffled.

'Hasn't the whistle gone yet?' he asked, a little crestfallen.

Several boys assured him that he was disqualified when he left the main ring, but the judge confessed he had totally for-gotten about his duties when the pony jumped the ropes. He decided that Tom and Glyn should ride it out between them, for the only other successful competitor had already gone home.

Glyn came bowling out, and his mount put on a creditable display of bucking and rearing in the middle of the ring. Glyn clung on well for a time, but began to slip gently further and further sideways with every jolt as the horse's feet thudded on the ground, and eventually his legs slid right off the animal. He was still clinging on to the mane with his hands, but was forced to leave go as the pony reared again, and stagger away, still on his feet but indubitably off the horse, well before the final whistle.

'Now my go,' said Tom with eager satisfaction. He was on to the skewbald and out through the gate almost before Glyn had begun to walk back.

'He does look like a cowboy,' said Tony, who with the other

younger boys had joined the group. He seemed to have decided to call a truce with Ruth, or else had forgotten all about
her outburst.

Tom did rather, as he swayed with the motion of the
prancing skewbald, his hands, not clutching the mane, but
waving above his head in imitation of the Western heroes. He
was staying on a long time; his chances looked good.

Suddenly the plunging horse put a forefoot in a hole, and
somersaulted violently to the ground. Tom was flung clear, but
landed with tremendous force on the arm he instinctively
crooked to shield his face. He rolled over almost instantly and
sat up, and then doubled up again on the ground. Several
people began to run across the field towards him, including
Kevin, and the boys followed.

Ruth stayed where she was, holding Tony from running out
after the others. 'There's no point your going,' she said. 'You'll
only get in the way.'

In due course Tom got to his feet and walked off in the
direction of the farm, helped by Kevin and followed by a posse
of hangers-on. Ruth went to join Pete, and was near enough to
hear Tom saying, 'I'd have beaten Glyn if the mucky old horse
hadn't fallen over. How long was I on, anyway?' Nobody knew
the answer to that, so Alan ran over to ask the judge.

'It were a draw,' said the judge, with unconvincing prompti-
tude. He could not be caught out twice having failed to keep
a proper check of Tom's attempt. 'Same time exactly. We'll
divide the prize.'

Alan ran back to tell Tom, but by that time Mr Thomas had
arrived with the car, and Tom was being helped in, so Ruth
could not see how he reacted to Alan's news.

'Has he broken lots of bones?' asked Tony.

'Done something to his arm, anyway,' said Pete. 'He was
holding it all funny.'

'A fracture, it is, no doubt about that,' said a woman nearby, who had been attending to Tom. She was a nurse from the local hospital so could be presumed to know what she was talking about. 'They'll take him straight to the hospital, so as they can X-ray him and that.'

Pete and Ruth stood about, uncertain what to do. Everything was over now in the main ring, and the remnants of the Annual Show lay about in the lengthening shadows like discarded Christmas wrappings. Stock-lorries and cars jockeyed for position to get out through the main gate on to the road, and Uncle Jack's rows of stakes and twine looked merely untidy, quartering out the tattered pasture to no purpose. Wherever the routes of vehicles had had reason to cross or converge during the business of the day, soil made threadbare patches in the grass, like a shirt showing through the worn elbows of an old pullover. The women collecting their exhibits from the competition tents looked hurried and fretful.

Up at the refreshment tents, the women were equally tired, but an air of relaxed good-humour prevailed. A few hundred satisfied stomachs left them in no doubt that their labours had been worth while. It had been a joint achievement, and no divisive rivalries splintered their collective contentment.

'How's Tom, then?' asked one of the helpers as Pete and Ruth and Tony passed by. For most of the show-goers Tom's accident had been no more than a moment of drama towards the end of a full day, and many had not seen it, or knew the boy involved, but the refreshment tent was a Thomas stronghold. Everybody soon realized that something was wrong when it was discovered that neither Mrs Thomas, nor Sylvia, nor the elder daughter Kate, were around to organize the soiled table-cloths and the uneaten cakes. They gathered around Pete to listen to whatever he could tell them.

Tony was very willing to tell all he knew and a good deal more, but found he was short of listeners. He turned irritably to Ruth. 'I'm starving,' he said. 'I bet you haven't gotten anything good for supper.'

Not only had she not got anything good, Ruth realized; she had not got anything at all. Cooking the occasional Friday Pie was all very well, but remembering that the housewife was expected to produce a meal at every mealtime was quite a different matter. It was not just Tony who had lived on sandwiches and ice-cream all day. There were also Pete and Uncle Jack to be fed, and Ruth realized she was starving herself.

She began to hurry homewards, Tony trailing behind and demanding that she wait for him.

'How can I?' she said. 'If you want supper when you get home, then you must give me a chance to get back and cook it.' Whatever could 'it' be? She couldn't call to mind a single thing in the larder of which there was enough to fill four hungry people.

Pete soon caught them up. 'I could eat a horse,' he remarked.

Ruth could not help laughing, for he could hardly have thought of a less cheering remark. 'Then you'd better go catch that skewbald,' she said, 'because I can't think what else there is to eat.'

Tony looked at her accusingly. 'I knew it,' he groaned.

Pete was unworried. 'We'll find something,' he said. 'I dare say Dad's got something. I haven't seen him for ages.'

Ruth realized she hadn't, either, not since he had come to the refreshment tent quite early on and taken a plateful of sandwiches and a cup of tea, and gone to watch the skittle alley as he ate them.

'He's been off somewhere,' Pete added in surprise, as they turned down the village street. The battered A-30 which had been stowed away in the garage beside the wheelbarrow when they left that morning was standing outside the gate. 'Or else he's just going.'

As they turned in at the gate, a delicious smell of cooking greeted them. When they opened the front door, Uncle Jack was sitting relaxed in his usual ancient armchair, and sounds of activity came from the kitchen. Pete looked at him inquiringly.

'Mum back?' he asked.

Uncle Jack nodded.

Chapter 5

WHAT had happened was that when Mrs Jenkins had gone to the hospital on Friday it was to discover that they had postponed the operation on Ruth's mother until after the weekend, so she had decided to make the complicated journey back home again. She had managed to get hold of Uncle Sam at the police-station on the telephone at lunchtime, just as she was about to catch her train from Bristol, and he had gone to find Uncle Jack, who had driven down to Newport in the car to fetch her. He had asked someone to tell Pete or Ruth what was happening, but the message had obviously gone astray.

'It makes things a bit difficult,' said Mrs Jenkins, 'because unless they operate on Monday or Tuesday I shan't be able to see her afterwards and get home again before you have to go back to work.'

'I should go Wednesday midday,' Uncle Jack admitted, 'if I'm to start work on Thursday morning.'

'And drive all night and then put in a day's work straightaway, handling them explosives?' said Mrs Jenkins.

'Well,' said Uncle Jack, 'if Sam can fetch you back on Wednesday evening, and I set off first thing Wednesday morning, Pete and Ruth can manage on their own for the day.'

'We can manage anyway,' said Pete. 'Not just for the day. For as long as you want to stay down with Auntie Sybil, Mum. Can't we, Ruth?'

'Yes, of course,' said Ruth. The prospect sounded rather fun.

'It's not Pete I'm worried about,' said Mrs Jenkins. 'Nor

you, really, Ruth,' she added hurriedly. 'But there's Tony, don't forget.'

Tony had disappeared with his precious burden of clay pigeons, to find a safe hiding-place for them. He had in fact forgotten all about them when they left the showground, but someone had found them while Pete was still up at the refreshment tent, and given them to him to take back.

'Oh, Tony's all right,' said Pete.

'Well, I don't know what's best,' said Mrs Jenkins. 'Come and have supper now, and we'll talk about it later. It depends when they do the operation, really, and how Sybil feels after it. And there's Patsy to consider. They'll be sending her home altogether soon, I shouldn't wonder. I was able to look in and see her today on my way in Newport, and she was looking very bright. Quite her old self.'

'Patsy?' said Tony, coming in. 'When do *I* get to see her?'

'Quite soon, love,' said Mrs Jenkins, absently. She had other problems on her mind.

It was a beautiful supper. Even after a long journey, and tired with accumulated worries, Mrs Jenkins could produce a meal that was in quite a different class from those Uncle Jack and Pete and Ruth had provided.

Next day Uncle Sam took Ruth down to see Patsy. The hospital said that she would be able to come home towards the end of the week, as soon, in fact, as Mrs Jenkins could undertake to be at home to look after her. Patsy, though full of enthusiasm for coming home, was more concerned about her mother than anything else, because she had not, of course, been able to see her at all since the accident.

'I'd much rather Auntie Mary stayed with Mom after her operation than came rushing back to look after me,' she said. It was not unreasonable; without her mother or father there, Auntie Mary's cottage in Llanwern was scarcely more home than the friendly hospital ward had become, where Patsy trotted about doing odd jobs for the other patients and joking with the young nurses. It would be good to be with Ruth, but Ruth was the one member of her close family she had been seeing fairly regularly at the hospital.

'What about this young brother of yours you've been telling me about?' asked the nurse. 'When are we going to see him down here?'

'But you said . . .' began Ruth, confused by this about-turn '. . . you said he too young to be allowed to visit.'

'Oh, not *now*,' said the nurse. 'I'm sure no one would mind. Just look at her.'

Ruth felt like saying, why didn't you say so, then, instead of waiting till we get all the way down here. There was not much likelihood of being able to get over again, with Uncle Jack going back to work, and Uncle Sam tied by police duties. It was just the same with her mother's operation. They seemed to think Auntie Mary had nothing better to do than flit up and down between mid-Wales and Bristol.

'I guess Tony wouldn't find it very exciting,' said Patsy. 'It would have been good to see him, though,' she added, a little wistfully.

Ruth could never understand how Patsy could feel that way about Tony, but her conscience pricked her over yesterday. 'He has missed you,' she admitted. 'He does keep saying he wants to see you.'

'Tony's quite all right,' said Uncle Sam firmly. 'Don't you start worrying about him, Patsy. Happy as a lark. I saw him yesterday, up by the clay-pigeon shooting with all his friends; having the time of their lives, they were.' He looked rather reprovingly at Ruth. 'The only thing for Patsy to worry about is getting herself well enough to come home again.'

Ruth and Patsy exchanged glances. Men could be very stupid sometimes, but they meant well, so there was no point saying anything. But if there was one thing that was evident, it was that the date when Patsy could come home had very little connection with how much she worried about her own health.

When they got back, Uncle Sam stayed for supper. He told them about the hospital allowing Tony to see Patsy. 'Which just shows they must think she's really better,' he said, 'not that there's much chance of taking him, but she'll be home soon anyway.'

Ruth wished he had not said that in front of Tony, but Tony, though he had evidently heard, because he looked across at Ruth, said nothing. His face was expressionless.

In fact, he had been so quiet and good all day, not making any fuss when Ruth had gone off with Uncle Sam, or complaining next morning when Mrs Jenkins began to prepare for another visit to Bristol, that his aunt was quite surprised.

'I must say, you all seem to have managed very well without me,' she remarked at breakfast. Certainly Ruth was a great deal more helpful than she had been before she went away, because she now knew what kind of things had to be done, and where the teaspoons and the washing-powder and the broom lived, and basic facts like that.

'Of course,' said Pete. 'Told you, didn't we?' He put another thick round of bread in the toaster. 'Did you think we'd just sit around and starve?'

'Not with your father around,' said Mrs Jenkins, 'but it'll be different when he goes on Wednesday morning.'

Ruth knew then that her aunt was going to be persuadable. Otherwise she would never have brought the subject up herself. Now that it was a serious possibility, Ruth was not quite sure whether she really relished the prospect of being left to keep house with no adult around.

'You needn't worry Pete will starve, any road,' remarked Uncle Jack, in that way he had of surprising everybody by coming out of what had appeared an inattentive silence with a comment that showed he had been with them all the time. He nodded towards the toaster, as Pete tried to extricate his toast, which had proved too massive to pop up properly.

'Not likely,' said Pete cheerfully. 'Anyway, you're not leaving us on a desert island. There's Uncle Sam just across the road, and the Thomases back over the field.'

'I could ask Sam to move in for a night or two,' said Mrs Jenkins. 'It's the nights I'm worried about. Not that nothing would happen, exactly, but I just don't like leaving Tony without a grown-up in the house; I don't think he'd like it, either.'

Pete and Ruth looked at each other. They both felt they would manage much better without Uncle Sam. He was used to doing for himself in his police house across the road, or coming in to his sister's for a good meal and some company from time to time, but he really would not know how to manage the children in their own house, and they would certainly not know how to manage *him*.

'I don't think he'd like that, much,' said Pete.

'He'd do it if I asked him,' said Mrs Jenkins, 'and be glad to help.'

That was just the trouble.

'Doesn't he get called out at night sometimes, or have to go on duty at night-time?' asked Ruth. 'It would be much worse having him get up and go off in the middle of the night than just being peacefully here on our own.' Her aunt seemed to be considering this, so Ruth, having had a moment to think, pressed on. 'I mean, on our own, Tony would go to bed in the usual way, and go to sleep while we're still messing around, and not feel any different. But if he was woken up in the middle of the night by Uncle Sam leaving, and maybe Pete and I would be asleep, why then, he might feel frightened, and make a fuss, and it would be difficult for Uncle Sam.'

'Tony could go to Tygwyn,' said Pete. 'Mrs Thomas would look after him.'

'Seems a bit hard,' said Uncle Jack, 'with Tom as he is.'

Tom had been kept in hospital over Saturday night, because by the time he had been X-rayed, and a fracture diagnosed, and the arm set and put in plaster, it was past midnight. However, he had been let out on Sunday morning, to be looked after at home. Pete had spent the evening with him, while Ruth was visiting Patsy, and had been quite surprised at how wan and tired he had seemed.

'If I know anything about Tom, he won't stay down for long,' remarked Mrs Jenkins, 'but I expect it will pain him a good bit at nights for quite a while. It wouldn't be natural if it didn't.' She thought about it for a moment. 'Still,' she said, 'it isn't as though she hasn't got plenty of helpers, with the two girls, and Gary would be there to keep Tony amused. I'm sure she wouldn't mind putting Tony up for a night or two, if I asked her.'

She went on turning it over in her mind, and Pete and Ruth kept silent, because they weren't sure what they wanted as regards Tony, and Tony himself was not in the room. He had finished breakfast and run out, because he said he had seen someone going up the road he wanted to talk to, one of the boys, probably, on an errand to the shop.

'But that would leave you two on your own here,' said Mrs Jenkins suddenly, her mind having gone off on another tack. Ruth had been thinking about this, wondering whether she might not feel a bit shy just with Pete, and no Tony for them both to talk to, or about. 'I don't know whether it would be right, that,' Mrs Jenkins went on.

'I can't see any harm in it,' said Uncle Jack, stolidly. Mrs Jenkins said nothing. 'But I think they'd be quite all right to look after Tony here, seeing as they can go to Sam or Tygwyn if they need to.'

'Well, I dare say it won't arise,' said Mrs Jenkins. 'If when I get down to the hospital this evening I find they've operated, I can spend tomorrow with Sybil, and I dare say they'll let me look in on her on Wednesday morning, and if she's getting on all right I can arrange with Sam to meet me in Newport that evening. But don't you leave it late setting off on Wednesday, Jack. It's a long old drive up to Scotland, and you're not to do it without taking time off to rest.'

So matters were left, and soon afterwards Uncle Jack drove his wife back down to Newport again to catch her train. Tony had not shown up, but Mrs Jenkins, in her unhurried methodical way, left the house all cleaned and tidy, and a casserole in the oven for their dinner.

Pete went off to see Tom, and promised to bring Tony back for dinner, if, as they presumed, he had gone up to Tygwyn with Gary. Ruth, bequeathed a clean house and no necessity to produce dinner, amused herself by experimenting with the recipe book. The domesticity bug had bitten her, and she set her mind to mastering this new subject with the same incisive single-mindedness that in the past she had reserved for subjects like history or mathematics.

'Sorry I'm late,' said Pete, unexpectedly, coming in as Ruth was putting a trayful of little cakes in the oven. She looked up, surprised, and saw it was half-past one. It was amazing how time melted away when a person was absorbed in something.

'I didn't know you were,' said Ruth. 'Where's Tony?'

It was Pete's turn to look surprised. 'I thought he would be home by now,' he said. 'He hasn't been at Tygwyn.'

'Not at all?'

'Not since I've been there, and nobody mentioned seeing him.'

'Do you think he's having dinner with Jimmy, or with Fish?'

'I wouldn't have thought so. I mean, their mums wouldn't let him stay unless they'd let you know, I shouldn't imagine.'

Ruth thought it unlikely, too. There was an unwritten law among the village boys that they could invite each other freely to play in each other's farmyards or gardens, but that at mealtimes everyone returned to his own.

'Oh, well, he'll come back when he's hungry,' said Pete. He could smell the casserole in the oven, and he was hoping Ruth would not want him to go and look for his young cousin before having his own dinner.

But at that moment, the door opened and Tony came in.

93

'Wherever have you been?' asked Ruth.

'Playing.'

'You're very late.'

'Sorry.'

'Who were you playing with so long? Didn't they go for their dinner?'

'It is late?' asked Tony, innocently. 'I didn't know. My watch has stopped.'

'Well, you should have asked,' said Ruth. Then she remembered she had been surprised at Pete's return, and decided to let the matter drop. 'Anyway, let's have dinner now.'

'Yes, let's,' said Pete.

'Have you waited for me?' asked Tony, quite surprised. Pete grinned, and Ruth changed the subject.

'Had we better leave some in the oven for Uncle Jack?' she asked, 'or will he get something out?'

'I expect he'll wait till he gets home,' said Pete. 'Better leave him some if there's enough.'

'It's your mother made this stew, not me,' said Ruth. 'She knows you.' She ladled a generous helping on to Pete's plate, and passed it to him.

He looked at it, without taking it. 'I never said stop,' he remarked.

Ruth added a couple of spoonfuls. 'That do you?'

'Be all right to be going on with. I'll be come back for more later if I want it.'

'Why you don't get fat beats me,' said Ruth. 'You're disgusting.' She began to dish out Tony's.

'Can I have less?' said Tony.

Ruth looked at him suspiciously. He had rushed out after a scanty breakfast, and it was well past his usual dinner-time. 'You all right?' she said.

'Yeah. Just not specially hungry.'

'I'll have this one, then,' and she put a little more on it, 'and you can tell me how much you want.'

'Hold it!' said Tony. Ruth passed over the modest helping thoughtfully.

'Tony,' she said, 'who were you playing with?'

'A friend.'

'Was it that man who lives in the wood?'

Pete looked up. 'Old Mossy?' he asked, with his mouth full.

Ruth seized the opportunity. 'Do you know him?' she asked.

'Yeah, I know who you mean. You often see him about.'

'Is he okay? I mean . . .'

'He's a bit simple, I suppose, if that's what you mean. Anybody must be, living in a leaky old shack like that.'

'Have you seen where he lives?' asked Tony, eagerly.

'Yeah. Went there as a kid. All the kids go there, sooner or later. It's a bit of a lark.'

'What's he like?' asked Ruth. 'I've seen his place – found it by accident the other day. He seemed very friendly, but he's odd, isn't he? You know what I mean?'

'Like I said, a bit simple. Little kids seem to like him, and I s'pose he likes them, else he wouldn't let them hang around.' He thought for a moment. 'Funny, though. It don't stop them teasing him when he comes into the village.'

'How, teasing him?' asked Tony.

'Well, you know, shouting names after him and that. And running up and making faces, and running away again.'

'That's mean,' said Ruth. 'Specially if he's asked them up to his place and been kind to them.'

'I know,' said Pete. 'But it happens. I remember going up there as a kid, looking for birds, and he showed me nests, and I went back, several times. I thought he was ever so nice.'

'Come up with me tomorrow,' said Tony. 'I'll ask him to show you the baby hedgehogs.'

Pete looked embarrassed. 'Better not,' he said. 'He don't like a lot of people trampling around.'

Tony watched him acutely. ' 'Cos you teased him after?'

'I know,' said Pete, 'it does sound horribly mean, when you

think about it. But when all the others are doing it, you don't think about it like that.'

'Did you?' said Ruth. She was surprised, for Pete did not seem that sort of boy.

'I was out with Tom and some older boys – we was in the top form at the primary just then – and we met him once, as we was all coming home together from school. And they all shouted, like in a chorus together, coming as close to him as they dared, and at first, I didn't say nothing, but it felt silly just staring when all the others were shouting, so I joined in.'

'What were you shouting?' asked Tony, half thrilled, half indignant.

'Oh, nothing special. Just "Old Mossy. Old Mossy", or something like that, over and over again.'

'That all?' said Tony, but Ruth could imagine how it must have been for the old man, with the hard boys' voices and the impudent boys' faces coming at him in mocking waves.

'It's not what you say that matters,' she said.

'At first, he just walked on, as though we wasn't there, and we kept just ahead of him, walking backwards and shouting. But when I joined in he looked at me real mad, and started to shake his fist, and then he looked almost as though he was going to cry, and he climbed over a fence in a great hurry and ran off across the fields. The other boys all leant over the fence laughing and shouting, but I didn't do that. But he wouldn't have known, because he never looked round.' He looked at his empty plate. 'I felt bad about it at the time.'

'And so you should,' said Ruth. She said it severely, not to be taken too seriously, because though it was a story to make her angry for the old man, she did not want Pete to think she was blaming him now. She wanted him to know that she realized a boy of fourteen was not the same person as he had been at eleven. She was scolding him for once having been that other boy, not for what he was now.

If Tony did that, she thought, I'd hate him, and feel sure

he was going to grow up into a horrible person; but it doesn't follow.

'Did you go back and say you were sorry?' asked Tony.

'No, I never went back,' said Pete. 'I don't think I've ever spoken to him since. Course, I've seen him around, but I don't know whether he remembers me.'

'Have some more,' said Ruth.

'I'm full,' said Pete, regretfully.

At that moment, Uncle Jack came back, and they talked of other things.

However, when Tony said next day that he would like to go and see Old Mossy again, Ruth said okay. She was pleased with Tony for asking, and wanted somehow to make amends to the old man for other boys' cruelties. She was glad, now she had heard Pete's story, that she had not timidly run away from the encounter in the woods. The recollection of the visit to the hedgehog's secret nest, and the shared meal, gave her pleasure now not so much for her own sake, but for Old Mossy's. As for Tony, it gave him something to do. Pete was spending a lot of time with Tom, because Alan was going back home that day, and Sylvia had asked Ruth if she would like to go with her and her mother to a farm sale near by. Uncle Jack had gone to do some work in the garden for the old grandparents who lived just outside the village.

That was Tuesday. In the evening, Mrs Jenkins rang Uncle Sam to say that Ruth's mother had been operated on that afternoon, and if the children felt they could manage on their own she would like to stay on for a couple of days. Uncle Sam was on duty on Thursday evening, so it was arranged that he would go down and meet her on Friday and possibly bring back Patsy at the same time, if the hospital agreed to allow her home.

When Uncle Sam called in to give them this news, Ruth was only anxious to find out how her mother was, and it was not until later that she wished she had thought of asking if Tony could go down with him on Friday, so that he could at least see

Patsy, and perhaps even be the one to bring her home. She herself intended to have a royal welcome for them when they got back, and show them how well she and Pete had kept the house running by themselves, and it would be easier to plan the event without having Tony under her feet, saying 'How soon will they be here?' all the time. That was not the only reason. During the past few days, when Tony had seemed so much more self-controlled and undemanding, Ruth had begun to think of him as more grown-up than she used to. People are very kind to him, and give him sweets and ask him to tea and spoil him, she thought, but I'd be mad if they did that to me instead of letting me go see Mom and Patsy in hospital. All the same, it's not surprising people treat him like a baby, because he does behave like one much of the time.

Because she was not sure whether Uncle Sam would agree to take him, she said nothing to Tony about her idea.

Next morning, Uncle Jack got up at four o'clock in the morning to start on his long journey back to work. Ruth had fully intended to get up and give him breakfast and fill his vacuum flask with tea, not because she did not think he could do it perfectly well himself – after all, he looked after himself all those long months living on his own in a caravan on a works site – but because she felt that was what Auntie Mary would normally do. However, though she set her alarm for five, by the time she got down he had gone, earlier than he had said, but he had told her the night before not to bother about waking herself up. He had washed up his cup and plate and swept up his crumbs, and the only sign that he had been in the kitchen at all was the still warm kettle.

Ruth crept back to her warm bed, thankfully if a little guiltily, and was soon fast asleep again. She was woken by Pete, standing in the doorway and calling her name.

'It's after nine, did you know?' he said.

Ruth did not know, not until she rolled over and looked at her clock, but she was mildly surprised that Pete should have bothered to come and wake her up. Tony, now, she would have expected, demanding that she get him his breakfast, but Pete was perfectly capable of getting his own.

'So it is,' she said sleepily. 'I'm surprised Tony hasn't come and bounced on me before this.'

'Tony's gone out,' said Pete.

'Out? He'll soon be back for his breakfast. I'll bet he's still in his pyjamas.'

'No, he's dressed and had his breakfast and everything, and gone. He's left a note.'

Ruth sat up quickly. 'You mean he did all that before you got up?' she asked.

'Well, yes, he must have. I only came down a few minutes ago, and found this note on the kitchen table.'

The discovery that Tony had got his own breakfast without telling anybody was almost more surprising than that he should have left a note and gone out.

'What does the note say?' she asked. Pete passed a scrap of paper to her. It had been retrieved from a waste-paper basket and its crumples partially smoothed out.

I have gone for a visit and will not be back till evening. Please dont tell Uncle Sam or anyboddy becuase I am okay Tony.

'Old Mossy, I bet,' said Ruth.

'That's what I thought,' said Pete. 'But why did he creep off so early? And not saying. It's not as though you haven't been letting him go.'

'I'd better get dressed and come down,' said Ruth.

Pete went downstairs. 'I've got some bangers cooking for me,' he called back. 'Shall I put some in for you?'

'No, thanks. Pete, do you think he could have ...? Oh, never mind, I'll wait till I come down.' It took so little time to slip on a shirt and some jeans that there was no point trying to carry on a conversation while she was running about the room upstairs and Pete had sausages sizzling downstairs.

'Do you think he could have made a plan with Old Mossy to see an animal or something, early in the morning?' she asked, coming into the kitchen a few minutes later.

'Like badgers, for instance?' said Pete.

'That would mean getting up early, wouldn't it?'

'Yes, very early at this time of year, because they'd have to be watching by the sett before the badgers were likely to be returning.'

Ruth glanced at the kitchen table. Unlike Uncle Jack, the remains of Tony's breakfast were plain to be seen – a cereal bowl that had contained cornflakes, a jammy plate, a badly-cut loaf of bread and a lot of crumbs and sugar strewn around.

'He certainly hadn't gone by five, because I came down then to see Uncle Jack off, and there was none of this around then.'

'Did you see Dad, then?' asked Pete, a little surprised.

'No, he'd gone. I was too late.'

'Anyway, if it was after five when he left, he wouldn't have been in time to see any badgers, or foxes, or anything like that.'

'He might have meant to go earlier, and not woken up,' said Ruth.

'Yeah, but that wouldn't keep him out all day. He says in the note he won't be back till evening. When I got up once to to look for badgers, I was back by seven, and had another couple of hours' sleep before a second breakfast.'

'I think I'd better go look for him straight after breakfast,' said Ruth. She filled herself a bowl of cereal and wandered about eating it and clearing Tony's things away at the same time. Pete made a pot of tea, and settled down to his sausages.

'I suppose he *has* gone to Old Mossy's, and not on some expedition with the other boys?' he said after a while.

'You were at Tom's yesterday. Did you hear Gary say anything about today?'

'No,' said Pete. 'No, wait a bit, yes I did. He was grumbling because Kate was going to take him into town to see the dentist. Could Tony have gone with Jimmy or Fish?'

'I don't think he's seen them since Saturday,' said Ruth.

On Sunday, so far as she could remember, Tony had stuck around at home all day, apart from volunteering, rather surprisingly, to go to chapel with Auntie Mary. No doubt he was glad to have his aunt home again, but he had not been particularly demonstrative about it. He had gone cannily in his dealings with Ruth ever since the Show, keeping an air of slightly distant politeness, and refraining from picking quarrels with her. At the back of her mind she had been a little uneasy about him, because the attitude was such an unfamiliar one for Tony but, between her visit to Patsy and her new-found enthusiasm for housekeeping, she had not given the matter much thought. Pete had spent a lot of time with Tom, and with Alan until he went home; Tony had been tagging around after him for most of the preceding week, and no doubt the novelty had worn off for both of them, because they had scarcely seen each other except at meal-times since Saturday.

The other younger boys had not sought him out either, and no doubt Mrs Thomas was too preoccupied over the weekend, with Tom, to think of inviting Tony to tea. During the first days after the accident everybody in the village had made a special point of being nice to Tony; it was not to be expected that they would keep it up indefinitely, now the main crisis was over.

All in all, Tony had solved the problem of how to amuse himself very conveniently by going off most of Monday and Tuesday to see Old Mossy. It was a longish walk, and Ruth had been surprised that he had been prepared to find his own way there, but it was only on Tuesday that he had had to do that. On the previous occasions she gathered that he had met Old Mossy in or around the village, and gone back with him.

On the first visit, at least, the old man had brought him all the way home again, too.

'He has been two days running, to Mossy, I mean,' said Ruth. 'Perhaps he thought I'd make a fuss about him going *again*.'

'Would you?'

'I don't know. I don't think I'd have bothered – it gives him something to do.'

'I still don't see why he had to go off at crack of dawn. I'll bet Tony's never got his own breakfast before.'

'You're right, he hasn't.' Nor have I, thought Ruth, until this last week, but there's no need to say that. 'I'd better get over there, and see what he's playing at.'

'Do you want me to come too?' Pete did not sound very keen.

'Not unless you want to.' She would have rather liked him to, but she understood his reasons for not wanting to visit Old Mossy, even after so many years.

'What'll you do if he's not there?'

'I can't think. Where else could he be?' Neither of them knew the answer to that, and Ruth felt a growing surge of anxiety, shot through with anger at being made to suffer it just as soon as the adult world had left them to fend for themselves.

'There's no point worrying about that now,' said Pete. 'Look, I'll come along with you part of the way, and I can wait down by the stream while you go and beard Old Mossy in his den.' That made it sound as though he were leaving Ruth to undertake something rather dangerous on her own, so he hurried to explain himself. 'I didn't mean it quite like that. I mean, you're not scared of Old Mossy by yourself, are you?'

'No,' said Ruth. 'Anyway, I gather he doesn't like too many people barging in on him.'

'Depends who,' said Pete.

They washed up the few breakfast things, more to prove to

each other that there was nothing really to worry about than because it mattered, and set off across the field behind the house. When they came to the bridge where the back road went over the stream, they crossed the lane and carried on beside the stream until it swung up into the little valley, and the woods began.

'I'll wait here,' said Pete. 'What will you do if you find him?'

'Wring his neck,' said Ruth.

'Yeah, but what after that?'

Ruth hesitated. It was only ten o'clock in the morning. It was one thing to vent her rage on Tony for choosing today of all days to play up, but quite another to have him sulkily under her feet for the rest of it for no good reason except revenge. As Pete had said, she had allowed him to spend all yesterday with Old Mossy, so it was illogical not to let him spend today, but it seemed rather weak to seek him out and then just say, 'Oh, there you are. Don't be late coming home.' But if Old Mossy was around there wasn't much she could say.

'It depends what he's up to,' she temporized.

Pete grinned. 'Well, don't go off hedgehog-hunting and forget about me,' he said. 'I did say to Tom we might both go up there and play Monopoly with him some time today – if you wanted to, that is.'

Ruth set off through the woods, pleased at the back of her mind that Pete had included her in his plans, but in the forefront was the dilemma about Tony. She pondered on the various things she would say to him. Then the thought recurred to her that he might not be there after all, and that she would only find Old Mossy going peacefully about his business. Should she tell him she was looking for Tony? In his note, Tony had asked her not to tell anyone. She did not feel particularly bound by that, because he had not consulted her first, but she did not want to bring grown-ups into it if possible, because it made her look so silly, after she and Pete had so earnestly persuaded Auntie Mary that they could manage perfectly well on their own. However, Old Mossy was different. He hardly counted as an adult, and he was not likely to go around telling other grown-ups about Ruth's troubles.

She stopped, and looked around to take her bearings. She would have expected to come upon the clearing by now, and began to wonder if she had gone wrong. She had only been there once before, and one part of the decayed woodland looked very much like another. She remembered that she had first found it by going right up to the fence that shut off the man-made forestry plantation, and that the old man's hut had looked as though it was one the foresters had used when they orginally planted the rows of conifers.

It could not be far from the forestry fence, so she worked her way diagonally upwards, retracing her steps slightly, until she came to the fence, and began to walk along parallel with it. She noticed one derelict shack almost as soon as she started, but it was not until she had walked past it and looked back that she realized it really was Old Mossy's. There was no feeling of habitation about the place, no smoke or smell of cooking, or sound of movement other than the scuffling of a blackbird in the leaves. She must have virtually walked round three sides of it without even noticing the clearing. It was the line of old rope tied between two trees that caught her eye, and then, when she came to look more closely, the ancient tarpaulin heaped under a tree that she remembered having noticed last time. She could not see the fire-place at first, and then realized she was almost standing on it – nothing but a blackened patch on the leaf-mould-coloured earth. Something like an outsize bat caught her eye, hanging on a branch beside her; it was the stretched skin of some creature killed and eaten so many rainfalls ago that now one could not tell whether it had once been bird or beast.

She shivered, for it was chilly under the ivy-hung trees, and advanced cautiously towards the hut. Surely Old Mossy could not be in there, silently watching her all this time? Or Tony, even? But she knew that Tony would not have kept quiet for so long. Once he had seen her, he might have hidden, giggling under his breath, but she had been wandering quietly close to this patch of the woods for a long time, and she was sure, if he had been about, she would have heard his voice long before she had got anywhere near the place.

She was suddenly engulfed in a fit of panic horror. Supposing, when she looked in through the darkened doorway, she came face to face, not with the innocent, weatherbeaten, slightly childish face of the Old Mossy she knew, but with a glaring, lunatic wildman of the woods, with eyes blazing like a fox surprised at its prey, hunched over the body of a murdered child?

She wanted to turn and run, run back to Pete placidly bird-watching by the stream, and drag him back up here to look first into the terrible hut. But she was Ruth, self-searching and reserved, the one who would have laughed coolly at her American girlfriends crying, 'Gee, weren't you scared?' Shaking in every limb, and scorning herself for doing so, she advanced upon the black hole that was the entrance to Old Mossy's home.

She stood there quite still for what seemed eternity, waiting to grow accustomed to the gloom. Something white caught her eye; it was not Tony's dead and upturned face, it was the enamel bowl from which Old Mossy had eaten his stew. What might have been a twisted body resolved itself into a clutter of rags that served the old man for a bed. One corner remained dark and unfathomable after all the rest had been purged of terror; she stared and stared at it until she saw it was simply nothing, just empty space going back to the cobweb-strewn wall of the hut – nothing except ... Nothing except a nodding spray of ivy that had infiltrated between the wall and roof and grown sickly in the obscurity.

Drawing a deep and shaky breath, she walked in and looked around. How little was necessary to support life! A roof, four leaking walls, an enamel bowl, a heap of rags, these were the only things to differentiate Old Mossy's way of life from that of the animals among whom he lived; for the rest, as for them, the woods were his larder, his kitchen, his living-room, his lavatory and his bathroom.

But there was one thing in the hut that was quite out of keeping with the starkness of Old Mossy's home. The bowl that had caught Ruth's eye was lying on an old log that presumably served both as table and chair; now she saw that propped behind it, leaning against the wall of the shack, was a childish drawing of some baby hedgehogs.

She had seen Tony drawing that picture only last night. 'That looks good,' she had said encouragingly, but he had half put his hand over it and said something about it not yet being finished. She had remembered, then, rather guiltily, that she had quite forgotten ever to say anything to him about the picture she had seen in the competition, or even to find out whether he had won a prize.

'I liked that picture of yours in the competition,' she had said then. 'Sylvia told me you did it up at Tygwyn. I never knew until then that you had entered anything.' She had waited, but he made no comment. 'I suppose it didn't win anything?' she might have added, but it was a bit late in the day to ask, and since she supposed Tony would have told them all if he had won a prize, she was pretty certain he could not have done. He had begun to busy himself again with his drawing, under his cupped hand, so she said no more.

If the hedgehog picture was now up in Old Mossy's hut, then Tony must have come up here this morning. She was sure it was the same picture. She took it out to the light and studied it, before propping it carefully up where she had found it. Then she went out, thoughtfully, and laid her hand on the site of the fire-place. The ground was still warm. Obviously Old Mossy, too, had still been here that morning. Did he always clear away the relics of his fires so thoroughly, she wondered?

She went over to the old tarpaulin and lifted it up, not so much scared now as intent on looking for clues. Under one end of it lay a pile of turnips, potatoes, swedes and onions, all higgledy-piggledy; at the other was a neatly-stacked pile of dry firewood, and an old fertilizer bag full of dead furze, wood-shavings and other firelighting material. It reminded Ruth of Girl Scout summer camps.

Then she ran quickly back through the woods to rejoin Pete.

Chapter 6

IT was not much of a day for August, cloudy and listless. August is not an exciting time of year for bird-watching at the best of times, and Pete was getting rather bored down by the stream. He had decided they were making a fuss about nothing and he would much rather spend the morning playing Monopoly with Tom than trailing aimlessly round the countryside looking for Tony. He hoped Ruth had found Tony with Old Mossy, had got her feelings off her chest and left him there; or, even if she did decide to bring him back with her, it would not matter much, because he could go off to Tom on his own then, and not feel he was neglecting Ruth. He would have been quite happy for Ruth to come and spend the morning with him and Tom ordinarily, but not if all the time he knew she was secretly fretting about where Tony had got to, and wanting him to abandon the game and go with her to look for him.

At that moment, Ruth reappeared. 'He's not there,' she said. Pete's heart sank.

'Did Mossy have anything to say?'

'He wasn't there, either. But Tony had been. He'd left a picture in the hut that I saw him drawing last night.'

'Oh, that's all right then,' said Pete, cheerfully. 'They've obviously gone off together somewhere, to look for some animals or something, like we thought.'

'Come up and have a look,' said Ruth.

Pete could not know how fearful a place Ruth had found it by herself.

'There's not much point in that, is there?'

'I didn't look round very carefully. We might find something to show where they've gone,' Ruth lied. She wanted Pete to go up with her to exorcise the devils.

'Come on, then,' said Pete. 'Let's be quick.' He decided that it might be worth going with her now to get her off his conscience for the rest of the morning.

It did not take them long now that Ruth was sure of the way and Pete kept up a hustling pace. He walked across the little clearing, felt the fire-place as Ruth had done, strode casually into the hut, noticed Tony's picture, strode out again, examined the carcase on the branch and the vegetables under the tarpaulin – 'Looks like Tygwyn stuff, mostly,' he commented – and added, 'Let's go back now; there's nothing here that's any help.'

Ruth could not tell him how scared she had been. He simply was not in that sort of mood. Silently she followed him back through the woods down to the stream, and so homewards.

Pete sensed her unease, but did not guess at the extent of it. He talked, to impose his own mood of cheerful unconcern on the conversation. If Ruth were to ask openly for his help he could hardly refuse it, so he determined that she should not be given the opportunity.

'Tony's pretty good at art, isn't he?' he remarked. 'I think that hedgehog picture was a lot better, really, than the one he won second prize with at the Show.'

Ruth digested this a moment. 'I never knew he won a prize,' she admitted after a revealing pause.

'Do you mean to say he never told you? 'asked Pete, surprised.

'No,' said Ruth. 'I forgot to ask, actually.'

'Oh, I thought you knew,' said Pete. 'You knew he'd put a picture in, didn't you?'

'Oh, yes,' said Ruth. She did not add that it was only because she had seen it on the table when going round the tents with Sylvia.

'Well, Gary took it back with him when they were clearing the marquee, because Tony wasn't going home then, and it was somewhere safe to put it, and I brought it back – let me see, was it yesterday, or Monday? I forget which. He was ever so chuffed about winning. I happened to be around when he and Gary first discovered he'd got a second, some time earlier on in the afternoon. Just before the sports, it must have been.'

'I don't know why he never told me,' said Ruth. She did, though.

'I'm surprised you haven't seen it. He's got it sticking up against the mirror in his bedroom, with the second prize card pinned on the corner. He said he was keeping it safe to show Patsy.'

Not me, thought Ruth, with a stab of hurt. 'I haven't been into his room this morning,' was all she said. 'If you remember, you woke me saying Tony had gone, and I never went up again after breakfast.'

'Must have been only yesterday I brought it back, then,' said Pete. 'I don't remember actually seeing it there when I went in this morning, but I wasn't looking for that. I looked in after reading Tony's note, before coming to you, just in case he was playing a trick, or had changed his mind or something.'

They walked on home in silence, Pete hoping he had turned Ruth's mind from thoughts of continuing the hunt for Tony.

Ruth herself did not know what to think. On the one hand she knew she would continue to worry until Tony turned up again. Her momentary terror up in the woods had left a residue of agitation in her mind, and her feeling that, ever since Saturday, Tony was behaving untypically, was reinforced by his actions this morning. It was so unlike him to go off, independently and secretively like that. It would have been much more characteristic of him to have woken her up and demanded that she get him his breakfast and take him wherever it was he wanted to go. If Old Mossy had suggested an early morning expedition to keep vigil over a badger's sett or something like that, surely Tony would have told her, and expected her to see that he set off at the proper time, properly fed? Or would he?

The only logical reason for going off like that was that he knew she would not allow him to do whatever it was he had planned. But what could he have planned?

'Could Old Mossy have taken Tony poaching?' she asked suddenly. Her knowledge of British game laws was hazy, and largely historical. Men were hanged in olden days for stealing the King's deer, but that, she felt, bore the same relation to the present situation as Tony's Western lore to the village rodeo. From a variety of folk-songs Ruth conjured up a picture of a battle of wits between the wily poacher and the gamekeeper, a surly figure with leather leggings and a long gun. Did game-keepers still shoot at poachers nowadays? And since Old Mossy walked openly across other men's farms with a gun and a dead rabbit or pigeon in his hands, what constituted poaching?

'Not if he wanted to catch anything,' said Pete, firmly. 'Any-way, if he were seriously poaching, salmon probably, he'd do it by night, most likely, with a torch and a gaff. But I shouldn't think Old Mossy goes in for that sort of poaching. That's done by people who can take the salmon to the towns to sell. Old Mossy just shoots to eat – maybe the odd pheasant now and again, or a couple of trout – tickles them, most probably, under the stones. I suppose he might be trying to teach Tony, but that wouldn't keep Tony happy all day.'

'Would Tony get into trouble if they were caught?'

'No, he wouldn't, but I suppose Old Mossy might. Anyway, if Old Mossy had promised to teach him how to tickle trout, or anything like that, he could do it any time Tony was up there, like yesterday or Monday; there'd be no need for Tony to get up at crack of dawn and go writing notes and such.' Then Pete remembered he was trying to soothe Ruth's fears, and tickling trout was as harmless an explanation of Tony's behaviour as any he could think of. 'Actually, I suppose he might; it would make it all seem more exciting. I'll bet it's something like that they're up to – something perfectly harmless really, but Tony thinks it isn't.'

Ruth did not reply. She knew how Pete felt about it.

She could not blame him. Seen from his angle, there was nothing particularly worrying about a nine-year-old boy getting up early and going out for the day on some private ploy. Well, perhaps not the whole day, but then it was quite likely Tony would come home long before the day was out, tired of the undertaking. He might even be home before them.

She tried to look at it from a grown-up angle, wondering, not for the first time, whether she ought to tell an adult. What would Uncle Jack have done if he were still here? Or Auntie Mary? Or even Ruth's mother? It was a difficult question to answer, for Tony's escapade would have taken on a new dimension if he had undertaken it when there were adults in charge. It was mean and childish of him to take advantage of the fact that there were not, but the fact remained, unalterably, that it was less momentous for him to slip out of the house without asking permission when the only bosses were Ruth and Pete than if he had done it when his uncle and aunt, or mother, were at home.

Even if he *had* gone off then, Ruth thought it was doubtful whether they would report the matter, say, to the police, at this stage of events. They would no doubt worry, the women especially, and send Uncle Jack out in the car to look for him, and ask around the likely households, but they would not go beyond that. The trouble was, thought Ruth, that for her the nearest available relation to consult *was* the police. Uncle Sam was in an awkward position; if he had been Pete's father, or her own father, then he would treat the matter first and foremost as a family affair; if he were merely the local policeman, then he would take official action as such. But he was in-between – an uncle at present standing in as a father, but without the close family sympathy of a father. The plain truth was that Ruth did not trust Uncle Sam to handle the situation in the best way.

Having decided in her own mind to say nothing to him, she asked Pete what he thought.

'No,' said Pete. 'We don't want him butting in. It would only make trouble all round, for Old Mossy too. Oh, don't fuss, Ruth. Tony will some home in his own good time.'

She would not have asked him if she had thought he was going to say anything different, but it was good to be reassured.

They had got to the back gate into the garden by then. Pete glanced across the field at Tygwyn.

'There's no point just hanging about here in case Tony should choose to turn up – he's not likely to before dinner anyway. Why don't *we* leave a note for *him* this time, saying we're up at Tygwyn?'

Ruth walked on ahead up the path. 'There's no point your staying,' she said. 'But I haven't made the beds or peeled the potatoes or any of that. I'd better not come.'

'I've made mine, as much as it ever gets done,' said Pete. 'I'll do the spuds if you like, while you do the beds, and then we can both go.'

'No, go on,' said Ruth. 'We've wasted enough time as it is. You'll never get a game in before dinner if you don't go now.'

'All right,' said Pete, 'if you're sure. I'll come back in good time for dinner. I bet if Mrs Thomas knew we were here on our own she'd ask us up for dinner,' he added wistfully.

'She'd wonder what we'd done with Tony,' said Ruth, and Pete had to agree.

'I'll keep a lookout for him,' he promised. 'Someone may have seen him around with Old Mossy, you never know.'

He trotted off across the field, and Ruth went into the house.

She went first to Tony's room and tidied his bed, and was rather surprised to see the jeans he had been wearing yesterday lying in a heap on the floor. She wondered why he was not wearing them today. He usually put on whatever came first to hand, which, unless someone had been in and put clean clothes out for him, was whatever he had taken off the previous night. She looked in his drawers to see what he was wearing instead, and the only trousers that appeared to be missing were his best pair. Trust Tony, she thought. He's got a perfectly good spare pair of clean jeans, but he doesn't think about that. His best pullover appeared to be missing, too, and when she looked under the bed she discovered his old one that he had been wearing with the jeans yesterday lying in a crumpled heap.

She went into her own bedroom and puzzled over it while making her bed. It seemed odd, even for Tony, to put on his best clothes in order to tickle trout, or look for badgers; in fact there was no possible occupation that Ruth could conceive of Tony finding to do with Old Mossy that required tidy, or even clean, clothes. While she was thinking about it, she realized that she had forgotten to look at Tony's prize-winning picture, and as soon as she had finished her bed she went back into his room.

There was no picture stuck up by the mirror, or anywhere else that she could see. He must have put it away in a drawer, which would explain why Pete had not noticed it that morning. She opened each drawer in turn, but there was no picture in any of them. She looked in the cupboard, and in all the places where it might have slipped down by mistake, and then back, more thoroughly, in all the drawers again. There was no doubt about it; the picture was not there.

Could Tony have taken it with him to show Old Mossy, as well as the hedgehog picture? It was a much bigger picture, unframed and on floppy paper torn from a drawing-book. It would not have been easy to take it up to the woods without spoiling it, still less to cart it around with him on whatever expedition they had embarked on, but he had not left the competition picture in the hut with the hedgehog one. He was unlikely to have thrown it away, or crumpled it casually in his pocket, because he had told Pete that he was going to show the picture to Patsy. Anyhow, the second prize certificate was still, apparently, atached to it, and surely Tony would have treasured that. He had been very pleased about winning, Pete had said.

Show it to Patsy . . .

Feverishly, Ruth hunted the house through for the missing picture, and all the time she visualized Tony, dressed to go out for the day in his best clothes, writing his note and setting forth at first light with his offering for Patsy under his arm. And I never said anything to him about going down on Friday to see her, she thought.

Eventually she gave up the search, and sat on the kitchen table to think. Had he really set out to go and see Patsy? Had he enlisted the help of Old Mossy? How was he proposing to get all the way to Newport and back in a day? Had he any idea of how far it was – seventy miles by road? Would Old Mossy know of a way of getting there, or agree to go with him? There were so many questions, and Ruth could not begin to answer any of them. And she juggled with them in her mind, making now one pattern of spinning question marks and now another, every so often she faltered as the thought recurred that Tony might not have had any such idea in his mind, and the whole airy edifice came crashing to the ground.

Sometimes she felt sure he had gone, and sometimes she dismissed the idea as nonsense. If he had not gone, then she wished he would turn up, so that she could divert her worry into a milk-churn full of rage and pour it all upon his head. But if he had gone, where was he now? And as soon as she thought of him silently discarding his family for their failure to listen to him, and turning to a half-witted old man to help him on a seventy-mile journey, her rage melted into something that was part fear, part admiration, and part compassion.

She wondered whether to go and consult Pete. The trouble was that one of the first things she wanted to ask him was whether he thought they ought to tell other people about Tony, and it was going to be difficult to get Pete by himself in the first place. Tygwyn was always a bustling place. She would have to go in through the kitchen, where Mrs Thomas and at least one, if not both, of the girls would be gossiping their way through the morning's work, to find him. More than likely, Tom and Pete and possibly Gary, home from the dentist, would be playing their game of Monopoly on the end of the big kitchen table, or else would be just through the doorway into the living-room. Ruth had never seen the door between the kitchen and the living-room closed. The life of the big family ebbed and flowed ceaselessly through it; in fact Ruth was not sure whether there was a door at all, or just a doorway.

Her main object in consulting Pete was to get, not advice, but information. He would know whether there was any prac-tical way of getting to Newport other than by car. There were no railways for miles around. A few local buses came and went from Aberafon, seven miles away, but no long-distance ones. The furthest anyone could get by bus from Aberafon was Pontargwy, twenty miles to the south, but that was only once a week. Pontargwy was a biggish town, by Welsh standards. There was a bus-station there, and no doubt regular services running to Newport, but she did not see how Tony was going to get to Pontargwy, or pay for a bus ticket when he did get there. Old Mossy seemed to live quite happily without money, though Ruth supposed he must have some. They could hitch-hike; but who in their senses would give a lift to Old Mossy? Tony by himself would soon arouse suspicion, and Ruth did not think he would dare to attempt such a journey by himself – she hoped not, in any case. Old Mossy and Tony together thumbing a lift along the main road would be a pretty suspi-cious-looking couple.

Old Mossy was so much a creature of the woods and fields, Ruth could no more imagine him boarding a car or a bus among strangers, and penetrating the city streets, than if he were one of his own hedgehogs. Would he really allow himself to be led into this sort of foray by Tony?

All this was getting her nowhere. She decided to go up to Mrs Burns' shop, where she had a feeling she had seen a time-table of some sort pinned up. She did not think it would be much help, but it was better than doing nothing.

As she went out of the front gate, she saw the Tygwyn car turning in the road by the shop, and then pulled in beside it, facing back the way it had come. Kate got out and went into the shop. Gary stuck his head out of the window and waved at Ruth as she approached; they were obviously on their way back from the visit to the dentist in Aberafon, and Kate had slipped on down into the village to get something from the shop before going home.

'Hi,' said Gary. 'I've just been to the dentist.'

'I know,' said Ruth. 'Pete told me you were going. What did you have done?'

Gary opened his mouth wide and demonstrated a couple of fillings. Then he shut it again to say something.

'Hey, Tony was feeling energetic this morning, wasn't he? Is he back yet?'

'Why, where did you see him?' asked Ruth evenly.

'Right up towards Llandewi-fach, with Old Mossy.'

'When was that, then?'

'Oh, about ten o'clock. We went round by that way, see, because Dad asked Kate to drop off some cup one of the farmers up there had won at the Show.'

The direct road from Llanwern to Aberafon lay along the valley, which was the way Kate and Gary had come back, a distance of seven miles. But another way was to take the lane up over the hill, the one that crossed the stream Pete and Ruth had followed that morning, and then rose up over the shoulder of moorland, where Ruth's father had taken his family for a picnic a few days before he was killed. A number of miles further along the road lay the hamlet of Llandewi-fach, perched in a wrinkle in the uplands, and further on still, the junction with the main road linking Aberafon and Pontargwy. Kate and Gary

117

presumably turned left, to Aberafon, at that point, making a journey of a dozen miles instead of seven; so surely anyone wanting to get from Llanwern to Pontargwy would turn right. On the day of the picnic, Ruth's father had driven to the T-junction in order to find a good place to turn; she remembered seeing the signpost there. Left, Aberafon, four miles; right, Pontargwy, sixteen miles. That would make a total of twenty-four miles from Llanwern to Pontargwy. It was an impossible distance for Tony to walk, Tony who was inclined to lag behind and grumble on the shortest family outing, but Old Mossy might not think so. Walking was how Old Mossy spent his day. He might not normally travel very far from his home in the woods, but he probably covered a good many miles just wandering about. It would not be beyond him to walk all the way to Pontargwy and back in a day, but what would he do when Tony tired?

'Which way were they going?' asked Ruth.

'Neither,' said Gary. 'They had got to the top, and were having a rest, probably, admiring the view and that, before coming down again.'

About a mile this side of Llandewi-fach, the road topped the final rise before sloping down into the village. The spot was one favoured by motorists for there was a level patch of moorland where they could pull off the road and brew tea or smoke a cigarette, overlooking the patchwork fields of mid-Wales; but Ruth did not think Tony had plodded all the four uphill miles on foot merely to admire the view and come home again.

'Funny, Old Mossy going all the way up there with Tony,' said Gary. He looked hopefully at Ruth, waiting for her to comment, but she said nothing. 'Kate didn't think it could be him, but I was sure it was.' Again, the statement sounded like a question.

'Probably was,' said Ruth smoothly. 'He said something about going on an expedition.'

Gary was still disposed to gnaw over a situation that had him slightly puzzled. 'Your auntie doesn't mind Tony going around with Old Mossy, does she?' he said. 'Lots of mothers won't let their kids go near his place; but my mum says that's daft, and he's all right. She gives him ever such a lot of things when he comes to our place.'

Kate was coming out of the shop, and Ruth turned to go home.

'You haven't been into the shop yet,' Gary pointed out.

Ruth had forgotten. There was not much point in studying bus timetables in and out of Aberafon now that she knew Tony was heading direct for Pontargwy, but she realized it would look odd if she did not go into the shop, as that was obviously where she had been heading, so she pushed open the door and asked for a bar of Tony's favourite chocolate.

As she ran home, she knew what she must do. She was going to borrow Pete's bicycle from the shed, and ride after Tony and Old Mossy as fast as she could. They had been walking for four hours now, assuming they had left Old Mossy's place by eight o'clock. At any rate, by ten they were only four miles away, which was not very fast going, but it had been all uphill. Old Mossy would expect to travel quicker after that, but Tony would be getting very tired, so it was unlikely they would have walked more than another four miles by now. It was a few minutes past twelve. That meant they would be about eight miles away, and by the time she had covered that by bicycle – say an hour – she would only be two miles behind them, and by then the road would be dropping sharply on the other side of the hills, and it would only be a matter of minutes before she came up with them.

She was not quite sure what she would do then, but felt she would have plenty of time to think that out as she was bicycling along. The main thing was to get going quickly, before Tony collapsed from exhaustion or Old Mossy decided he was bored with the whole operation. They could, of course, simply have called it off and started back for home, in which case she might meet a disgruntled Tony round the first corner, but if she did there was no harm done. On the other hand, they might have almost reached Pontargwy, or been given a lift there, in which case they could already be on a bus to Newport. Ruth had a feeling it might be a long time before she got home again, and she had better take some food and warm clothes with her.

There was also the question of Pete. She would have liked his company, but she wanted his bicycle more, and there was the continuing difficulty of getting hold of Pete privately – particularly now that Gary would be at home. Also at the back of her mind she had a half-formulated idea – an unnaturally bold and illogical one – an idea she did not wish to take out and examine until she was safely on her way; but one that she was sufficiently aware of to know that Pete would not agree with it. She decided to write Pete a note. He must think it's a habit of our family, she thought.

She got everything ready first, part of a sliced loaf and a hunk of cheese, two apples, some biscuits and her home-made cakes, and a plastic bottle of water, and the bar of chocolate, and her polo-necked sweater and anorak – she noticed as she took it down from behind the door that Tony had taken his best one and left the old one behind – and stuffed them all in Pete's saddle-bag, apart from the anorak, which she clipped on to his luggage carrier. It occurred to her that Pete's bike was the only real luxury he possessed. He had saved up Christmas and birthday money from all his relations for two years in order to buy it, and had been lucky to get one, second-hand but almost as good as new, with every accessory including the saddle-bag and carrier and, most useful of all, three-speed gears, for his thirteenth birthday a year ago. He cared about it a lot; Ruth hoped he would not mind very much about her taking it.

She went back into the kitchen, found a sheet of paper and

a pen, wrote PETE in large letters on one side and turned it over. She fiddled impatiently for a few moments with the corner of the blank page, wondering what to say; then she wrote: – 'I am sure Tony is trying to get to Newport to see Patsy. Gary saw him on the road with Old Mossy and he has taken his best clothes and the competition picture. I have borrowed your bike and gone after them. Hope you don't mind. Can you disguise our absence from Uncle Sam?' She thought for a bit, then went on: 'I don't know when I'll be back, but have taken some money. If I'm not home by seven, I'll try and telephone the call-box between then and half-past seven, so could you hang around there? Sorry about all this. Ruth.'

She thought about the money while she was writing, and as soon as she had finished she went up to Mrs Jenkins' bedroom and took a wallet out of the drawer. It gave her a strange feeling, for it had been in her father's pocket when he was killed. Someone had taken it off him and handed it to Mrs Jenkins. Ruth had been with her aunt when she had told her mother about the money, and her mother had asked her to use it to help pay for the children's upkeep. Auntie Mary had replied no, she wouldn't do that unless she had to, because Sybil might need the cash to help tide her over until their money affairs had been sorted out. Ruth knew that hitherto her family was more comfortably off than Pete's, for an American lecturer's pay was a great deal better than a construction worker's, but she did not quite know about the future. Nobody had mentioned that, and it had not occurred to Ruth that they might find themselves very poor now that their father was dead, until this moment. The fact of her father's death struck her with a new finality as it dawned on her that if she took five pounds out of the wallet, there was no one to put another five pounds into it again.

Although sobered by the thought, she did not feel guilty about taking the money, because her mother would obviously wish her to spend it, if she had to, in order to get Tony safely home again, but she resolved to bring back as much as she could. Thinking about money in this realistic way for the first time in her life, Ruth found herself wondering just how Auntie Mary was managing to feed her and Tony as well as Pete, and keep up these constant journeys to Newport and Bristol. She thought: oh, well, Mom will be able to pay her back afterwards, and then; after what? For it often seemed to Ruth, now that the first shock of the accident was over, that her father's death was somehow a temporary thing; after a while, it would unhappen, and they would all return to their old New York life together.

She counted out the five notes, saw there were still fifteen left, and put the wallet carefully back, thinking that Tony would never again have his mother at his beck and call, for she would have to go out to work and leave Ruth in charge for much of the time; not just for a few weeks, as now, but every day. Had Tony realized this, and not she, when she had held their relationship over his head, menacingly, like a sword, during their quarrel at the Show?

She went quickly downstairs, her face set, put the pound notes carefully in her own purse at the bottom of the saddle-bag, and rode off down the deserted village street.

Chapter 7

BICYCLING was one of the few athletic pursuits Ruth reckoned to be good at. About three years ago, it had become one of her father's crazes, and Ruth and Patsy, who until that time had asked in vain to be allowed to have bicycles, suddenly found themselves each presented with smart new models, and together with their father they bicycled miles through New York streets and New York parks. He would have liked to take Tony and his wife in tow, too, but she had refused to agree to Tony, who was then only six, being sacrificed on the perilous streets to his father's latest enthusiasm. Tony and his mother stayed at home, but for three months Ruth and Patsy were plunged into a new and adventurous world, seeing their familiar environment from an unfamiliar and sometimes dangerous angle, and penetrating, too, into parts of the city they had never been to before. Their father declared that bicycling was good exercise, good for the muscle and circulation and brain alike, that it developed initiative and independence, that it was the only answer to New York's traffic problem, the only one that cost virtually nothing and that did not poison the atmosphere.

All these facts remained true after the three months had elapsed, the only inconstant factor being Mr Crane's interest, which waned as suddenly as it had begun. The family returned to polluting the atmosphere and neglecting their muscles, for Mr Crane was studying Russian, and he did not feel it safe for his daughters to bicycle about the city without him.

Ruth swept round into the narrow lane that ran alongside

the stream until it joined the bigger road coming down past Tygwyn, and swung sharp right, pedalling fast and dropping into bottom gear in order to let her momentum take her as far up the hill as possible. She determined not to dismount until she had reached the cattle grid, nor did she, but by the time she got there her breath was coming in gasps and her heart was pounding, and the bicycle, weaving from side to side of the road in order to ease the gradient, made no faster progress than if she had been walking.

She got off thankfully, and pushed on doggedly up the hill that seemed to stretch ahead of her for ever, although in a car it had not seemed very long. After a bit she left off looking ahead, but leaned on the handlebars watching only the steady progression of gravel beneath her feet while she counted a hundred paces. Then she would look up, take heart at the lengthening slope behind her, and plod on, head downwards once more until another hundred paces had been counted.

She did this six times, with a short break in the middle when the ground had eased out sufficiently for her to ride. As she looked up for the sixth time, she knew she was within sight of the top, but what caught her eye was not anything that marked the crest of the hill, but a movement about halfway down the slope towards her. It had looked like a figure slipping unobtrusively over the bank and disappearing down the steep slope of the open hillside on her left. If she had been counting a hundred and one paces instead of a hundred she would have missed seeing it.

The figure could have been that of a farmer, out after his sheep, but it seemed to be moving too furtively for that. It could have been a hiker, but the colours were wrong; the walking holiday-maker usually stood out in the landscape he had come to admire, by virtue of his yellow oilskins or his scarlet knee-socks or his striped bobble-hat. It could have been a pony, or a sheep; but there had been something purposeful about the sudden descent. Ruth knew it was Old Mossy.

She dropped her bicycle and ran to the edge and looked down. There he was, moving diagonally across the slope, already on about the same level as she was.

'Hi!' she called. She wished she knew what his proper name was. The absurd compromise, Mr Mossy, rose to her lips, but she hastily suppressed it. 'Hi!' she called again. 'It's me. Ruth!'

He seemed to half glance in her direction, but only went on walking, a little faster and veering more downhill. He obviously knew who she was, and had already seen her on the road before she saw him. Ruth's heart gave a plunge as she realized he was deliberately avoiding her, partly because she was sure she could not catch him if he really meant to run away, and partly because it made her wonder what he had to hide. She began to run down the slope at an angle to cut him off. At first he just carried on, but as soon as he began to veer away, she stopped. It was like trying to catch an unwilling pony.

'Please,' she said, softly, for they were not far apart now, 'please wait a minute. There's something I want to ask you.'

He slowed down, looking at her reluctantly. She began to keep pace, so that he would not think she was trying to corner him, but only to talk to him.

'How are the hedgehogs?' she asked.

His face took on an odd expression, part irritable, part embarrassed; then he shook his head slightly, and walked on.

'Will you let me see them again one day?' she asked. She wanted to run and shake him, shouting 'Where's Tony? Where's Tony?' but she knew that would be like slamming a door.

'Perhaps,' he said, still walking.

It was a small victory for Ruth, for she had got him to answer. But she wished she could stop him walking, because all the time they were going further and further away from the bicycle. 'Can you stop a minute?' she asked, 'because really I was on my way up to the top when I saw you, and there was something I wanted to ask you.'

He paused then. 'The hedgehogs is all right,' he said shortly, and hurried on down again.

'Oh, good,' said Ruth. 'But there was something else, too. I think my brother was going to go up this way this morning, and I wondered, if you'd been up there, whether you'd seen him.'

He turned and walked straight towards her, and she could see the muscles of his face tensing under the scrubby grey hair. Mrs Thomas says there's no harm in him, Mrs Thomas says there's no harm in him, she thought to herself, and tried to keep her own face relaxed.

'I just thought you might have,' she said mildly. 'I was going to give him a lift back down on the bicycle, or he'll be late for his dinner.'

'I ain't never set eyes on your brother,' said Old Mossy. 'I got to get back to feed them hedgehogs.'

'Of course,' said Ruth. 'You know who I mean, Tony, who's been coming up to your place.' She saw denial on his face, and added, 'The one who drew the picture of the hedgehogs.'

'I ain't done nothing to him,' said Old Mossy. He began to stride away again.

Ruth ran after him desperately, and caught him by the tattered sleeve.

'I know, I know,' she said. 'I only want to know where he is. I've lost him, and there's no one to look after him, only me, and I can't find him.' It was only when she felt her own lips trembling as she spoke that she knew how close she was to tears.

He pulled his sleeve out of her grasp and dived away straight down the hill. Ruth sat down heavily where she stood, defeated. She thought he had gone out of view, because her eyes were clouded with unshed tears, and she climbed to her feet again to clamber wearily back up the hill. But she stopped, surprised, when she heard his voice, and realized he was standing not many yards away, still and grey as the wind-bitten hawthorn behind him. He was not looking at her, but he was talking aloud, whether to her or to himself she was not sure.

'Them as climb mountains has got to be willing to take what the mountain gives,' he said. 'He didn't ever ought to have gone; she shouldn't ever have let him go.'

'I didn't know ...' Ruth began, but he went on as though she had not spoken.

'She shouldn't have let him. She should have told him Mossy'd got to feed the little 'uns; else they'll come out for what they can find, and the old fox will get 'em. I told him Mossy'd got to go back now, got to feed the little 'uns, but he don't take no heed. Don't leave me, Mossy, he says, but Mossy's got to. Can't walk further than he can walk back before the little 'uns get hungry, and come out, with their spines all soft, when the old fox is about. I promised her, I said to him, I promised her as lay flat on the road with the owls eating her, she trusted me; she knew Old Mossy would look after the little 'uns. She shouldn't have let him go, to be up there worrying Old Mossy with his crying like a rabbit that's got shotgun pellets in its foot and can't keep running; Old Mossy don't like to hear the crying, got to get away, got to get away to feed the hedgehogs, they're the quiet ones; they don't make much noise, hedgehogs don't.'

'Where?' said Ruth. 'Where was the crying?' She had been trying to follow the flow, to guess when the 'she' referred to herself, and when it was the dead hedgehog mother he was talking about. Now he had run into silence, and she prompted him with great caution. If Tony had been left crying on the side of the main road between Aberafon and Pontargwy he would certainly have been picked up by now, unless he had gone to seek help at a house. 'Was it by the roadside?'

Old Mossy shook his head. 'No, no,' he said, with surprising directness. 'Not the new road, the big road that goes round and about, with all them cars and lorries. You don't want to go that way, not if you're walking. It's much quicker the green way, but you've not got to be afraid of the dark trees. It's not right, they shouldn't let him come, him that's afraid of the dark trees. There's nothing in the trees to scare you, I says to him, they're not like the lorries and the cars with the strangers in them, going to the towns full of strangers; but he's not afraid of the cars and the lorries, that's the way he wants to go, and it's no use wanting to go that way if Old Mossy goes with you, I said to him; if you get in them cars or lorries, who knows where they're going to take you, I says to him, and so we took the green road. But the hedgehogs started to cry, and Mossy had to come home.'

'So you left him in the dark trees after the signpost to Pontargwy?' asked Ruth.

'Oh, aye, after the signpost, for the dark trees is all on the other side of the big road, from the mountains,' said Old Mossy.

'Was he still crying when you left him?' asked Ruth.

'I put a stop to the crying,' said the old man. 'I couldn't hear it no more; only the hedgehogs I hear. Don't you fret, little 'uns. Mossy's close at hand now.'

Suddenly he was no longer visible against the grey tree; Ruth looked about, and saw him slipping away into the fringes of a straggling spinney of hawthorn, of which the tree near where he had been standing was an outpost.

'How do you mean, you stopped the crying?' she shouted after him, but he turned his head away and began to run. It was useless to try and catch him; even if she succeeded, he would not be in the mood to tell her any more.

Doggedly, she scrambled back up the hill, clutching at the short stringy grass with her fingers for her plimsolls tended to slip backwards in the steep slope. She regained the road more quickly than she had expected, for she had felt she was going down and down when pursuing Old Mossy, but in fact it was not so very far, although when she reached the road she found she was a good deal lower down than where she had left the bicycle.

She was aching and breathless by the time she came to it, but the hill was already levelling out and a few moments of determined pedalling brought her to the crest, and she was able to free-wheel down into the hamlet of Llandewi-fach.

There was another hill on the other side, but not such a daunting one, and she was soon making good speed along the level upland. Long before she reached the T-junction, she could see the lorries and cars traversing the naked moorland ahead of her, following the main road from Pontargwy to Aberafon, and it did not seem very long after leaving Old Mossy that she found herself at the junction, standing by the signpost she remembered from the day of the family picnic.

Here Ruth stopped and puzzled over Old Mossy's directions, if such they could be called. According to him, they had not followed the main road to Pontargwy, 'the big road that goes round and about', but had crossed over and taken a short cut that led off on the opposite side from the mountains. But there was no obvious track visible from where she stood, and she did not know whether to turn left or right along the main road to start looking for it. The road junction lay at a saddle in the moors; her own road had been following a ridge which dipped slightly at this point, and then rose towards a bluff overlooking the lower ground to the south; the main road ran from the east over the moorland, across the head of her road at the dip, and then sloped away westwards down the flank of the mountains until it reached Aberafon, lying hidden by a further fold at the foot of the range. Roughly, she reckoned Pontargwy lay to the east, Aberafon to the west, she had come from the north, and southwards the grassy moorland sloped upwards to the bluff.

For a few minutes she debated whether to follow the Pontargwy signpost and hope for the best, or whether to spend more precious time in climbing up to the top of the bluff in order to get a better view of the area. In the end she took a coin from her pocket and tossed for it, heads for the road, tails for the bluff; it showed heads, whereupon, illogically, she knew she had wanted all along to go up the bluff, and to prove that she was not superstitious, she went.

It took rather longer than she had expected, and twice she nearly turned back, but she made herself go right on to the best vantage point. and she was glad she had done so, for now the whole country lay below her like a map.

The most important discovery was that Pontargwy did not lie the full sixteen miles away due east, as she had rather naively assumed from the direction of the signpost, but directly below and beyond her, glittering and smoking in the centre of the variegated green plain. She could follow the line of the road from where she had left the bicycle by the progression of vehicles on it; it went out of sight behind another shoulder, then reappeared lower down the same shoulder, which it then proceeded to descend in a series of hairpin bends, and finally disappeared from view in the woodlands of the lower slopes.

The whole of the sweep between the hill upon which she was standing and the further shoulder was filled with a forestry plantation; the upper limit of this vast furry cloak, hemstitched with a stout fence, lay only about fifty yards below her, and reached as high upon the opposite side; at the head of the gully it lapped along the verge of the mountain road, and at its lower edge it appeared to be bounded by the same road, several miles further along its circuitous length, and the best part of a thousand feet lower.

Ruth could not see much of her own side of the valley, for it was hidden by the nearer trees, but she could see that the further side was criss-crossed diagonally by straight forestry roads. They looked grey and stony and new, but running like a backbone from the road at the head of the valley downwards till the nearer trees hid it from view was an older looking trackway, green and inviting; a pathway from the uplands to the plains for walking men since before the Romans came, a ribbon of whinberry and heather and mosses and ferns left among the poor cardboard conifers by the forestry men, perhaps for convenience or sentiment, perhaps because at this very heart of the valley would be a living stream, dried to a few moist patches in the summer, tumbling abundantly in the winter, defeating the foresters' trade.

That must be the green road, thought Ruth, and she guessed that in two or three miles it would emerge again at least half-a-dozen miles further along the main road from where it had left it.

Where was Tony? Was he huddled somewhere down that green lane between the fir trees, too tired to go further, or after resting would he try to retrace his steps to the top road, or press on down to the bottom, where in either case he would no doubt soon attract the attention of a passing driver? Or would he try and take a short cut back on to the main road by following one of the metalled tracks that very possibly crossed it down in the dip of the valley where Ruth could not see? She would not allow her mind to return to Old Mossy's words, 'I stopped the crying'; earlier that morning, standing outside the old man's hut, she had let her fears stampede her, and she did not intend that to happen again.

All the same, she turned and ran back down the tussocky slope to her bicycle. She knew she was hours behind Tony, and the five minutes saved would scarcely make much difference to him, but it was five minutes less to keep panic at bay.

Once she was back on the road, it was only a mile of downhill cycling to the head of the valley. The road curved round and continued following the contour of the hill for the time being; she could no longer see where it began the series of loops that brought it eventually down to the plains below. Here, on her left, the green road fell away between the fir trees, and here, somewhere, Old Mossy had turned for home to feed his hedgehogs, and left Tony, exhausted and tearful, on his own.

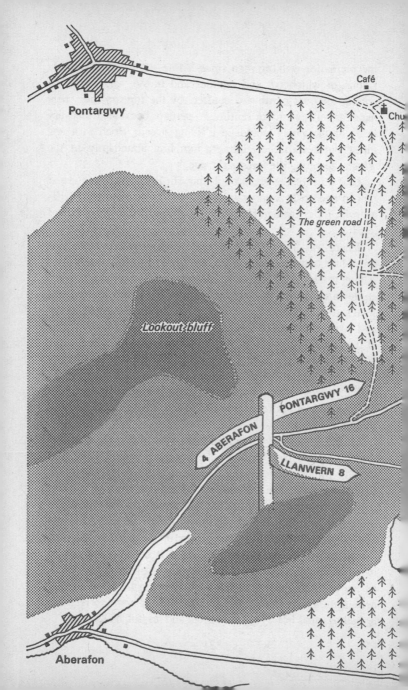

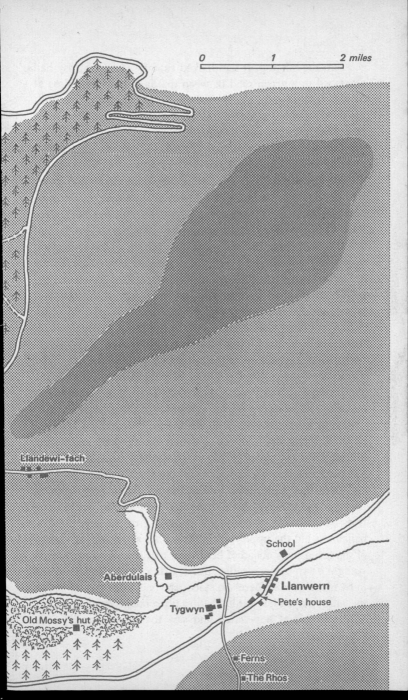

From the hill-top, it had looked exactly as Old Mossy had described it, a green road between the dark trees, but close at hand it did not seem like a road at all. The highway was built up on an embankment at this point, and a wide drain-pipe protruded through the shale beneath it, to act as a culvert for the rain-water from the hills. There was no stream running now, in August, but from the scatter of bare boulders immediately below the drain-pipe it was evident there was water running down it for much of the year. Below that, the stream-bed disappeared beneath clumps of whin and heather; there were boggy patches, marked out by blotches of reeds and broad-leaved beige grasses, sometimes hiding rocks, sometimes squelching hollows of peat; gorse grew freely wherever the ground was dry enough, and further down Ruth could see the path was swathed in bracken, just now at its thickest and tallest.

She had been wondering, as she came down the main road, whether to take the bicycle with her, for the sake of its usefulness should she emerge at the lower end without having found Tony. Now she realized it would be an impossible burden, so she lowered it, with some difficulty, down the embankment and tucked it in among the firs at the side of the green way.

The fir trees had been with her for the past half-mile as she pedalled along the highway, but only on her left, and as the hillside fell away steeply from the banked-up road, she had not felt particularly conscious of them. Now she realized how tall and dark they were, how lifeless the needle-carpeted ground between the trunks, how narrow her view of the world. The trees on each side of her made a corridor of the sky, the embankment hid the upper hillside from her sight, and the curve of the green track ahead of her meant that she no longer looked straight down into the valley, but at a short strip of path walled in by more trees. Where she stood, she was in sunshine, but as the valley curved leftwards, shadow filled the green road.

She looked at her watch and saw that it was nearly four

o'clock. She realized that the hollow feeling at the pit of her stomach was not just caused by anxiety; she had not eaten anything since breakfast. Immediately it struck her that she was setting off down the hillside leaving all the food and clothes on the back of the bicycle, and she scrambled back to retrieve them, but, apart from taking a couple of biscuits to keep her going, she did not stop to eat anything then, for Tony might be close at hand and she did not want to risk missing him. She had a problem, because she had stuffed everything loose into the saddle-bag or on to the luggage-carrier, and without the bicycle had no means of carrying it. However, she managed by unbuckling the saddle-bag and taking that with her, and tying her anorak round her waist.

An hour later, she stopped and ate some bread and cheese, and drank from the stream which now had a trickle of water in it. She had not come out at the other end of the wood, and she had not found Tony. She untied her anorak and put it on, partly because the bracken and brambles kept tearing at it, and at her unprotected arms, but mainly because now the trees shut out all the light and she was cold. It was a chilly day for August, and beginning to look like rain. Although she was going downhill all the time, progress was far from easy. At first she had been scrambling down precipitous and stony ways, or plunging along through the whin and heather, unable to see where each foot would find firm ground, or squeezing round bogs, gorse scratching her ankles or fir trees scratching her face and neck. Lower down, the pathway filled up with bracken, and though pressing blindly through the clinging green curtain was a pleasant change at first, it soon grew tiring. Now there were brambles, too, sending long and vicious runners in among the bracken, to tear at her unsuspecting hands as she sought to swim through the fern, or catch her round the shins and send her stumbling to the ground. It was where the brambles grew thickest, however, that she had her first real confirmation that she was on the right track.

All the way down through the bracken she had looked for signs that someone else had breached a path through the greenery, and sometimes she thought they had, and sometimes she was not sure, for there were a myriad tracks running short distances through the fern and then disappearing off into the plantation on one side or the other – made by foxes or hares, perhaps – and other places where large areas of bracken had been flattened, but that might have been caused by a sudden gust of wind on the rain-sodden fronds after a storm. Besides, where the bracken was not thick, a boy and an old countryman could find a way without leaving an obvious track, and where it grew close and high Ruth herself could see nothing outside her own green capsule. But then she came to a clearer patch, where willow-herb made a splendid splash of pink among the dark trees, and hid a growth of virulent nettles that sought out the gap between her jeans and her plimsolls, already scratched and sore from everything else she had walked through; on the far side of it the whole pathway seemed blocked by a thick barricade of brambles. Studying it dolefully, Ruth noticed a narrow entrance into the tangled mesh, where the arching sprays had been trampled down, or bent back and tucked into the undergrowth. She stepped cautiously through, and saw that the pathway went purposefully on, and where the runners had been broken the frayed edges were fresh and green. This track had definitely been made by human beings, and quite recently.

It was just beyond the bramble patch that she came upon a forestry road, cutting a stony swathe through the regimented trees. It swept down from the right, swallowing up her bosky path as it crossed diagonally, and away up the opposite slope to the left. Beyond the interruption, her path resumed its way on down the cleft of the valley, and the trickle of water re-emerged from another culvert. In the middle of the metalled road lay something blue. It was Tony's second prize certificate.

Ruth picked it up and, holding it in her hand, called 'Tony!

Tony!' A pigeon flapped noisily out of a fir tree and circled off with beating wings. Then all was still. She called again. It was an eerie experience, to stand there at the heart of an empty forest, surrounded in every direction by trees as far as she could see, with just a cross of grey sky above her head and a grey road crossed with green at her feet, and hear nothing but her own voice calling. The dark trees seemed to be watching her, waiting to march in from the four quarters, and swallow her up where she stood, a diminished figure shouting in a tiny voice at the centre of the cross, with a blue card in her hand.

She remembered Old Mossy. 'She shouldn't have let him go, him that's afraid of the dark trees.'

Afraid of the dark trees. Afraid of the dark trees. Afraid of the dark trees.

The sky was getting darker, too.

As Ruth stood there, looking at the blue card, she felt sure that this was where Old Mossy had turned back.

But what had Tony done? If he had enough strength left in him to go anywhere at all, she would have expected him to struggle back after Old Mossy, anything rather than be left alone, as she now stood alone, under the dark trees. Perhaps he had sunk down here, exhausted, and Mossy had slipped away unnoticed and Tony had looked round later to find himself alone; where would he have gone then? On down the green track, or up the diagonal forestry road to the right, hoping to come quicker to the busy road again that way? It would depend on what Old Mossy had told him about how much farther he would have to go before reaching the lower boundary of the forest. That was something Ruth wished she knew the answer to.

She shouted again to the impervious regiment of trees, and then took out the bread and cheese. There was something homely and comforting about the plain food, and as she chewed she felt less forlorn. Either she grew a little taller, or the trees grew a little shorter; at any rate, the sense of menace receded.

The trees were but trees, and she an active girl perfectly capable of walking to the perimeter of the forest in whichever direction she chose. 'There's nothing in the trees to scare you,' Mossy had said, and he was right.

Though she ceased to be afraid for herself, there was little to allay her fears for Tony. If he had the sense, and the strength, to follow any one path to its conclusions, he would almost certainly come out somewhere near civilization, but it was a big 'if'. Ruth herself had experienced a gust of unreasoning panic; she knew that even with Old Mossy, Tony had been 'afraid of the dark trees'; how much more so when Mossy had gone, and he was alone and less able than Ruth to reason with his fears. He might run blindly along every turn that offered itself, or even up and down the same track, like a dog left behind by a car after a picnic; or, worst of all, he might leave the tracks altogether, and wander through the woods themselves. It would not be too difficult for him, for the trees were well-established and nothing grew beneath them once one had pushed through the weakly undergrowth skirting the edges. Only the dead lower branches made a network of face-stinging mesh, but even Ruth could keep below this by crouching, and for Tony it would be easier.

She knew it would be madness to turn in under the trees and search at random, for the trunks marched across the land in solid echelons for square mile after square mile. If she sought outside help, a search party could dispose of the various forestry roads in an hour or so, but it would take days for even a large body of men to cover the solid acres of the plantation.

The thought that she could seek outside help blew in on her like a fresh breeze. Originally, when she and Pete first discovered that Tony had gone, it was a possibility she had considered and temporarily rejected, but since she had set out on the bicycle she had left off even thinking about enlisting the help of outsiders. She realized Tony himself might have done so, in which case the whole affair would come out into the open; but until she had completed her own mission, successfully or unsuccessfully, she felt that this was something between her and Tony and Patsy. There was a private world of their own to set to rights, and it could not be done by inviting a horde of adults to trample over it.

All the same, the adult world was there – it was something she had almost forgotten – and if Tony was really in serious trouble, then the sorting of their private world must wait, and she only had to walk to the nearest house or telephone with her story and a host of policemen and doctors and forestry workers and the like would step in and organize her life for her.

Fortified by this realization, and by the bread and cheese, she set out once more upon the green track. At first it continued in much the same way, partially choked with bracken and brambles, but as the path descended towards the plains, the trees grew taller and sturdier, and the light that filtered through into the ride dimmer. The bracken died away altogether, and the brambles grew less dense. The ground was covered with long thin green grass, and clumps of stately foxgloves; then there were shining stretches of bluebell leaves, slippery to walk on, the pale seed-heads few and far between in this unlit glade. The slope of the path was much less steep than before, and in places it was almost level. Ruth realized she had come right down off the hill, and wondered how long it would be before she came out on to the main road.

She wished the sun were shining, for it was impossible to keep a sense of direction in this deep corridor among endlessly repetitive trees. As long as the path was descending the hill, she had felt she knew more-or-less where she was, because she had observed the line of the valley from her viewpoint on the bluff, but now she had no guideline. The path seemed to meander, turning first to the right, then to the left, and she suddenly realized that the little stream had disappeared. There were various ditches cut at angles from the ride into the plantation, and the rivulet must have been diverted into one of these.

From the top of the hill she had not been able to see the lower edge of the forestry; she had only deduced that the green road ran almost directly through it from the road at the top to the road at the bottom. Perhaps it did no such thing, but merely wound about to some irrelevant corner of the wood, miles from where she wanted to get. Old Mossy had not said that the green road went all the way; he might have intended to cut through the trees at some point. In fact, Ruth now began to persuade herself that she was walking parallel to the main road, and skirting westwards round the base of the bluff upon which she had stood.

As she rounded the next corner, her fears appeared to be realized for the path, instead of bearing right and losing ground again as she had hoped, dropped into a little hollow and then rose steadily on the other side, as though once more climbing the hill.

There, in the dip, lay Tony.

Chapter 8

IN an instant, all her earlier fears flooded in upon her. Tony lay curled among the foxgloves, his face hidden, his legs drawn up to his chest, his red anorak a discordant blotch between the pink spikes, still as a dead rabbit.

I must just keep walking till I get there, thought Ruth, for dread threatened to root her feet to the ground, while anxiety urged her to run forward at full pelt. So, apart from a strange rigidity about her movements, she kept going steadily onward as though nothing had happened.

At last – it seemed an age, though cannot have been more than a minute – she stood beside him, and stooped down, not daring to touch him, but trying to see some part of him that was not covered in clothes. Then she heard the rhythmic husky breathing of a child with a cold, or who has fallen asleep crying, and felt the sobs of relief rise in her own throat. She stepped quickly round to the other side of him, and sat down. She could see part of his cheek now, and his mouth, slightly open, with the loosely curled fingers of his left hand just touching his lips, as though he had gone to sleep sucking them as he had used to do when he was small, and they had fallen away in the relaxation of sleep.

She felt his hand, and his cheek, to see if he was cold, and he turned his head. She could see the criss-cross pattern of grasses on his face where he had been lying. Then he opened his eyes and looked at her, at first without surprise, as though he were in bed and she had come in to tell him to get up for breakfast, then with puzzlement as recollection dawned.

'Tony,' she said, 'are you okay?'

'Ruth!' he said. 'How did you find me?' He rolled over on to his hands and knees and fell clumsily upon her, crying out in sudden agony as he did so.

'Tony!' she exclaimed. 'What's the matter? Are you hurt?'

'Foot's gone to sleep. Ooh, ah!' He rubbed it tenderly.

'Oh, is that all?' Ruth spoke in simple relief that he was neither stabbed nor strangled nor maimed, but Tony was indignant.

'It darned well hurts,' he said, and indeed he was half crying as the life flowed painfully back into his cramped leg.

Ruth laughed and hugged him. 'I'm sure it does,' she said. 'Only I thought you might have a broken leg or something.'

'It couldn't hurt more if it was broke,' said Tony, 'but it's getting better.' They both sat in silence side by side while Tony wiggled his foot about cautiously until the pins-and-needles receded. Then he said, 'Why are you here?'

'I came to look for you,' replied Ruth, and began to tell him what had happened, but broke off to say, 'Why, you're shivering.'

Even in August, the shady ride was a cool place to go to sleep on the dank grass, and it was not surprising that Tony felt chilled; his face looked pinched and colourless.

'I'm cold.'

'Have something to eat; that should warm you up.'

'Have you got something?' Tony's voice betrayed incredulity, as though a fairy godmother had descended on him with a bag full of wishes.

Ruth laid out all the food. Apart from the bar of chocolate, it wasn't very exciting, but there was plenty of it, and Tony made no complaints. They shared it between them, for Ruth was as hungry as her brother. While they ate, Ruth told him how she had found him, but she forbore from asking him any questions for the time being.

'I never thought you might come and look for me,' he said, at length.

'Why ever not?'

'I didn't think you'd bother. I just thought you'd be hopping mad when I came back.'

Ruth made no answer.

'I did want to see Patsy.'

'I know. I was going to ask Uncle Sam to take you on Friday.'

'Really?'

'Yes, really. Do you want this apple?'

'Yes, please. Have you got one for yourself?'

'I ate it earlier. Tony, what did you think was going to happen if nobody came to look for you?'

'I don't know. Lie down and die, I suppose.'

'Tony!'

'Only kidding. I guess I'd have woken and found my way to the road. It can't be much further, only I couldn't go any further. I just couldn't.'

'It's lucky it's summer-time.'

Tony shivered and looked around. 'I hate these trees. They seemed to be all chasing me. I tried to tell Old Mossy, but he wouldn't listen. He *wouldn't* listen.' His voice rose tremulously as the scene came back to him, and Ruth hugged him again silently. She knew what he meant about the trees.

'Tony,' she said after a while, 'when Old Mossy went back home, what happened?'

'He just went. I told him I couldn't go any further, and he just *went*.' Tony considered this shattering reaction; in his experience, grown-ups did not do that sort of thing. Children might, but grown-ups, never.

'Were you crying?'

'A bit. A lot, as a matter of fact. I . . . I was scared.'

Ruth carefully plucked ten foxglove blooms from the spike beside her and studied them, cupped in her hand.

'Old Mossy told me he stopped your crying. What did he mean by that?'

'I don't know. I went on crying a long time after he'd gone; till I went to sleep, I suppose. He just put his hands over his ears and ran away.'

So that was it. 'It stopped it for him,' she said.

'Yeah,' said Tony. 'That would be like Old Mossy, wouldn't it? I should have known better than to trust him, but I couldn't think of anyone else.'

Ruth tipped the foxglove cups out on her knee. She picked up Tony's left hand and carefully fitted a pink bloom on each finger and thumb, then did the same with his right hand. He watched, quiescent, till she finished the job and then crooked his fingers, laughing.

'I'm a lion, with bloody claws. Grrrrr!'

'Funny-coloured blood. I think you're more like a dragon, with your red anorak.'

'I wish I was. I could fly out of this wood, then, and take you with me on my back.'

'Tony, did Old Mossy say anything about how far it was down to the other end?'

'He didn't say anything useful at all. He's like – oh, I don't know, he's weird. He'll talk away about something he's thinking about, or he'll listen when you're talking to him, but he doesn't answer, if you know what I mean. You can't have a sensible conversation with him at all.' He leant across and looked at her watch. 'Hadn't we better get going?' he asked. 'It's six o'clock.'

'Yes,' said Ruth. 'I guess we had. I was just wondering which was the best way to go.'

'You mean, instead of going all the way back through this ghastly wood we could go out this way to the road, and try and get a lift or something?'

'Something like that. There's Pete's bike up at the top still.'

'Well, if we had a lift that far it would be something. Couldn't I ride on the carrier when we have the bike?' Ruth was silent, so Tony added, 'I know you're not meant to, but it's a darn long way. It's mostly downhill from there, so it wouldn't take long on the bike, but with one of us walking we'd be terrifically late getting home, and it would be dark, most probably.'

'Is that what you want to do most of all now – get back home as soon as possible?'

Tony looked at her in surprise. 'What else were you thinking of doing?'

'I was just thinking that having got so far it seemed rather a pity for you not to see Patsy after all.'

Tony's surprise deepened to astonishment.

'But ... but you wouldn't let me do that, would you? How, anyway?'

'How were you proposing to do it?'

'Well, I was going to have Old Mossy take me to the bus-station in Pontargwy, and then take the bus to Newport. I've got the money for my ticket.'

'Where from?' asked Ruth, for he looked suddenly guilty.

'I borrowed it, sort of.'

'Where from?'

'Don't be mad if I tell you.'

'Go on.'

'Well, you know that wallet that used to be Dad's ...'

'You got it from there.'

'Yeah.'

'How much?'

'It was rather a lot. You see, I thought if I was going to take any, I'd better take enough.'

'How much did you take?'

'Two pounds.'

'That's not a lot. I took five.'

She watched the expression on his face change from the

slightly mutinous look of someone about to receive a row into a startled grin of conspiracy.

'You didn't!'

'I had to get the money from somewhere, and goodness knows where you might have landed up before I found you.'

'So now we can both go together to see Patsy?'

'It was just a sort of idea I've been having. But you must feel beat after all this. We could try to get back home, with lifts and the bike, like you said, and hope no one has found out anything, and I'd try and persuade Uncle Sam to take you on Friday, like I was going to anyway.'

'But if we don't go home they're bound to find out.' This was a situation quite new to Tony, in which he and Ruth were allies against the rest of the world. Sometimes he and Patsy got into mischief together, but more often Patsy and Ruth were accomplices and he an aggrieved outsider, likely to go and tell Mom, just as he had always taken it for granted that Ruth would take up the position of the disapproving adult whenever she discovered him in the act of wrong-doing. Now she seemed to be the leader in a scheme more adventurously far-ranging than anything he had envisaged.

'Not if we can find a telephone kiosk before half-past seven.'

'What's that going to do for us?'

Ruth explained about her note to Pete. 'If I can get hold of him on the telephone and explain things, perhaps he could stop Uncle Sam from discovering we weren't home, or anybody else who calls in.'

'And what are we going to do?'

'It's a lot nearer to Pontargwy than it is to Llanwern. If we can get there fairly quickly, we can find somewhere to stay, and then get the bus to Newport some time tomorrow morning, go and see Patsy in the afternoon visiting-time, and get the bus back after.'

'And walk home?'

'We'll have to think about that,' said Ruth, for that was as far as her ingenuity had gone. 'At least we won't be any worse off than we are now, and we shall have seen Patsy and you will have had a night's rest. You really don't want to walk all the way home from here now, do you?'

'Not if I can help it,' said Tony, but after his sleep and his meal, and with Ruth for company, he felt quite a different boy from the forlorn and exhausted Tony of three hours ago.

Ruth got to her feet and held out a hand to him. 'We'd better get going,' she said. 'It really matters about that telephone call, because if I don't get hold of Pete he may get the wind up, and tell Uncle Sam. And we still don't know how much further we have to go.'

Tony scrambled up. 'What will happen if Pete does tell Uncle Sam?'

'I dread to think,' said Ruth. 'With any luck, he'd come out and look for us in his car, and maybe find us walking into Pontargwy.'

'Why with any luck?'

'Well, if he doesn't find us, or thinks he might not, he'll probably make it into a police affair, and have search parties out for us.'

'I wondered about that when Old Mossy went off and left me. I thought, I guess someone will come and find me before I die of cold and starvation. I never imagined it would be you, though, not just all on your own.' He trudged on in silence for a few moments, and then said, 'I was terrifically glad it was you, though. But I still don't understand why you're not hopping mad about me going off this morning without telling you.'

'As a matter of fact I was,' said Ruth. She grinned. 'But it got worn out before I found you.'

'I'm darn glad you didn't find me sooner, then,' said Tony. 'This is going to be good fun. I was getting a bit worried, even before Mossy took off, about finding my way around in Newport on my own.'

'And well you might,' retorted Ruth, but she knew he would have felt a lot more confident, urban child that he was, in the crowded streets than the lonely forest. 'What I can't understand is how you ever thought you were going to get there and back in a day.'

'I suppose it was a bit stupid,' said Tony. 'I thought Mossy would help me get a lift, and then wait in Pontargwy for me to come back on the bus.'

'Did you ask him?'

'You know what he is. Like I said, he doesn't answer, exactly. But he didn't say no, so I thought he would. I never thought he'd just walk out like that.' After a pause, he added, 'You won't tell Mom about this, will you? She'd be ... she'd be madder with you than me, wouldn't she? She'd be mad with both of us.'

'If we don't find civilization soon, it's going to be out of our hands. No, of course I won't tell her, not yet, not until we both think it's okay.'

'Which will be in about a hundred years,' said Tony. 'Ruth, if they *do* find out, and send out search parties and suchlike, there's no need to let on you've agreed to come with me, and spend a night away and all that. They can just think you're bringing me back home, and we've gone this way because we thought it would be quicker. We did think of that, remember?'

'That's not going to help you much.'

'No, but just because I'm going to get into trouble anyway there's no need for you to be in it too. It would be a lot worse for you, because you're older.'

'Being older doesn't always make a lot of difference,' said Ruth, thinking of the afternoon before they heard that Patsy was conscious again, and Tony had sounded so callous about her unhappiness, saying it was easier for her because she was older.

'It does in this case,' said Tony. 'You'll probably get in a row anyhow, for letting me run away in the first place.'

'I'm glad,' said Ruth, 'you're beginning to realize it isn't always fun to be the oldest.'

'It isn't always fun being the youngest either,' said Tony. 'You don't have to run away to get to see your own sister in hospital. Or Mommy either. Anyway, if we're caught this evening I won't say anything about you planning to go on to Newport with me.'

'Thanks,' said Ruth. She was about to add, 'I should hope not, considering the trouble you've caused me already,' but then she thought, I'd only be saying that because that's the way I'm used to talking to Tony, I don't really mean it, and she shut up.

'Why was it Patsy you specially wanted to see, not Mom?' she said, thinking about his last remark.

'Don't be dumb,' said Tony. 'Bristol's too far away, and anyhow Auntie Mary is there. And Mom would die of a heart attack if I turned up to see her all on my own, you know that.'

They were all good practical reasons, and Ruth was surprised just because she had never imagined Tony thinking along such logical lines.

'Why didn't you ever tell me before?' she said.

Tony looked at her in disbelief. 'I did, hundreds of times, till I was sick of hearing you tell me not to be a baby – though why it's being a baby when I want to do, just once, what you keep doing all the time, I don't get.' It was a cry of bottled-up resentment, and the sentence ended on a strangled note.

'I see,' said Ruth, slowly, because she did see. This independent and perspicacious Tony was the same child as the tiresome boy interrupting her private world with cries of 'I want Mom'. It was as though over not just the past weeks, but for years, they had been standing on opposite sides of a window writing messages to each other which, seen from the wrong side, came out all back to front, as garbled nonsense. But mirror-writing can be deciphered, even from the other side of the window, if one takes the trouble, she thought.

A lot of possible answers occurred to her, but she could not make up her mind how to express them, so she just said, 'I *do* see,' and put her arm round his shoulder.

'That's what Patsy does,' said Tony, allowing her arm to remain there for a companionable moment before shrugging it off.

Yes, thought Ruth, Patsy doesn't bother much about words when she's talking to people; she looks and laughs and does, and those things show through a window-pane without getting turned back to front in the process. People think I'm clever because I can use words, but what are they good for except possibly exam papers?

'Look!' said Tony. 'There's the edge of the forest!'

The firs marched tall and straight on either side of them, as they had done for miles, for another fifty yards, and then they stopped. Elder saplings and brambles grew in the aperture, but through and beyond them Ruth and Tony could see patches of an unconfined sky. They hurried forward, pressing impatiently through the undergrowth, to emerge on the roadside.

For a moment they stood in sudden disappointment, for this was no major road, but a modest lane, tarmacadammed, it is true, but untended-looking, and a faint green film of moss growing down the centre proclaimed that few vehicles passed this way, and those that did needed the width of the lane for their wheels.

The only building in sight was a small and ancient church, backing like a nervous animal into the encircling woods, keeping them at bay with a low wall, crumbling and ivy-covered, which marked out the untended graveyard.

Ruth and Tony looked to left and right, wondering which way to go.

'I hear traffic!' said Tony suddenly, and they stood still to listen.

Unmistakably, a lorry was approaching at a fast speed; the sound grew louder, and as quickly receded; then came the lighter hum of a passing car. Obviously a main road lay not far away, but which way?

'Let's try to the right,' said Ruth, and, 'I think it's this way,' said Tony, turning left, at the same instant. They laughed, and then broke off to listen, for a heavy vehicle sounded as though it drew up almost opposite them. Their own lane appeared to be sunk below a high bank, overgrown with blackthorn and other impenetrable scrub, on the side opposite the plantation, so that they could not see in the direction they wanted to go, but on both sides of them the lane curved outwards.

'I know,' said Ruth. 'You go left, and I'll go right, and we'll stop before we lose sight of each other and shout if we see anything.'

Tony started off at a run, so Ruth ran, too, but stopped before she had gone thirty yards. She had come straightaway within sight of the main road, and lorries fleeting past, and turned, triumphant, to summon Tony.

'Come here!' she called. 'It's this way.'

But Tony was waving, too. 'It's *here*!' he yelled. 'I can see the road!'

Then the truth dawned. The lane they had come out upon was little more than a lay-by, probably a loop of the old road, which had been by-passed in a more recent road-straightening scheme. It had only been kept up to allow access to the tiny church.

'You go your way, I'll go mine!' shouted Tony.

'Okay!' called Ruth, and they both ran ahead. As Ruth puffed up the steep little incline on to the big new road, she noticed a faded and lopsided notice, with an arrow pointing the way she had come, saying LLAN-SANTFFRAED CHURCH. She could see Tony running towards her along the verge, about two hundred yards away, but something else had caught her attention. On the opposite side of the road stood a new-looking filling-station, where a huge articulated lorry was just beginning to draw out. It must have been the one they heard stopping. At one side of the main building was a lorry-driver's pull-in café, and at the far end, just off the ample forecourt, a letter-box and a telephone kiosk stood side by side on the grass verge.

'Hey, I've found something,' said Tony, as they met opposite the filling-station.

'Seen the telephone kiosk?' asked Ruth.

'Say, so it is. Our luck's in. That café's open, too.' He looked hopefully at Ruth, but she did not respond, so he went on, 'Come see this.'

He led her back to his entrance on to the road, and pointed out an old milestone, embedded in the bank of what used to be the main road. Carved into it, almost indecipherable, and obscured by hedgerow plants, were the words Aberafon 17 Pontargwy 3.

'That's not bad,' said Ruth. 'We must have cut off miles. No wonder it seemed such a long way through the forest. We could walk that. I've been worrying rather about getting a lift.'

'Yeah,' said Tony. 'Mom'd have a fit if she knew.'

'That's New York,' said Ruth. 'Around Llanwern it's different, because everybody knows everybody, but this ... this is different again.' The impersonal traffic hurtling past, the ugly functional filling-station, seemed a far cry from the village street. 'But there's another thing: someone might pick us up who'd want to know too much. It'll be the same when we look for somewhere to spend the night.'

'Couldn't we camp then? You know, sleep in a barn?' That sounded exciting, something to talk about afterwards.

'I was wondering about that. It would be safer, in some ways, and save a lot of money.'

'And we could buy food over there. Oh, do let's do that thing. I wish there was a barn just here, because we can easily walk the three miles tomorrow morning.'

Ruth looked at her watch. It was ten past seven. 'Let's go phone first, anyway,' she said.

'Why not in the church?' said Tony.

'Because there's more likely to be a public telephone in a call-box than there is in a church,' said Ruth.

'I mean sleep in it, stupid.'

'Why, yes. Yes. I guess we could, at that. Don't you think it would be rather cold and spooky?'

'I'm not scared of spooks.'

'I bet you would be if you were there on your own.'

'Bet I wouldn't. Bet I would,' he added hastily, as he caught Ruth's sceptical glance. 'Bet you would, too. But if we're together it will be okay. Anyway, a barn might be spooky, too. Lots of rats.'

'You were the one who wanted to sleep in a barn.'

'Yes, but the church is nearer.'

'You just don't want to have to walk any further.'

'Do you?'

'No.'

'Well, then. Anyway, I think it's going to rain.'

Certainly the sky was getting darker.

'Tell you what,' said Ruth. 'If by the time we've phoned Pete, it's raining, we'll definitely go for the church. But if it's cleared, we'll carry on for a while.'

'Don't forget we're going to eat first,' said Tony.

That was sensible, because they were not likely to find anywhere else open this side of Pontargwy, and even in the town it might be quite difficult to find a place to stay, if they didn't get there till eight or nine o'clock.

'Okay,' said Ruth. 'First we'll phone, and then we'll eat, plenty . . .'

'Okay,' said Tony.

'. . . because we don't know when we'll eat again, and then we'll decide about sleeping.'

By now they had crossed the road and had reached the kiosk.

'Hey, there's someone in there,' said Tony.

'Darn it,' said Ruth, looking again at her watch. This was a complication she had not anticipated. It was now quarter past seven.

The man in the kiosk – he looked like a lorry driver – talked for a full twenty minutes. After the first five, a few drops of rain began to fall. Tony and Ruth began to walk round and round the kiosk, so as to be sure the man really knew they were waiting. After ten minutes, it was raining so hard they were driven to seek shelter in the doorway of the café. Tony read the menu hanging on the door. After a quarter of an hour, Ruth went and glared through the window of the kiosk, rain streaming down her nose and making rats' tails of her hair as it hung out from the hood of her anorak. The man grinned, blew her a kiss, and went on talking. She stormed back to Tony.

'It's so stupid!' she raged. 'There's Pete waiting all this time at Mrs Burns, and if I don't get through to him in less than a minute, he'll go and tell Uncle Sam everything.'

'Do you think he will?'

'I wouldn't blame him if he did. After all, anything might have happened to us. Oh, get on, man!'

'I'll tell you something,' said Tony. 'I'm not walking three miles in this rain. Please? Hey! he's out.'

The man strode towards the café door, hunched against the rain. 'It's all yours, kids,' he said cheerfully, and disappeared inside. Ruth had already run to the kiosk and caught at the heavy door almost before it had closed. Feverishly she dialled the number, and listened with growing despondency to the bell ringing out hollowly in the kiosk at Llanwern. Then, just as she was about to put the receiver back, Pete's voice said, 'Hullo?'

Chapter 9

'Oh, Pete,' said Ruth, 'I was afraid I'd missed you. I've been trying to reach you for hours.'

'I know,' said Pete. 'There's been some girl in here for ages and ages. She's only just gone. Natter, natter, natter. I could have strangled her.'

Ruth giggled. 'That's funny. No, I've not been calling you because there was a guy in this one, driving me up the wall.'

'Talking to his girlfriend in Llanwern, most probably,' said Pete. 'But that's not the point. Have you found Tony?'

'Yes,' said Ruth. She told him what had happened and then, rather hesitantly, what they were planning. Having Pete on the other end of the line made her realize that there was precious little in her scheme that was likely to commend itself to him. He was not going to get any of the fun, he would have to spend the night on his own and be left with all the responsibility of seeing that no one discovered their absence.

'Yes, but . . .' began Pete, and Ruth could only feel how unreasonable she was being. But Tony was pressed wetly against her in the narrow space of the kiosk, looking up at her with a trust that was an entirely new element in their relationship. She could not let him down now.

'I know,' said Ruth. 'It's not much fun for you, but honest, we couldn't walk back till we've had a night's rest, and if we wait until tomorrow anyway, we might just as well go and see Patsy as come back first thing.'

'Yeah,' said Pete. 'I'm not complaining about the fun –

much. But the point is everybody's going to be around asking us to do things. Mr Thomas said today why didn't we all go up there for a meal, and Uncle Sam is due back from duty any moment now, and he's bound to come round to our place. If I can't produce either of you for two whole days everybody will think I've murdered you and buried you both in the back garden.'

'Well, if they find out, you can't help it,' said Ruth. 'Just put them off for as long as you can.'

'That's all very well,' said Pete. 'But if Uncle Sam looks in this evening and I say Tony's having a bath and you're in the toilet, and then by tomorrow I have to come clean and say actually I haven't seen either of you for twenty-four hours, it's me that's going to be in the soup, not you.'

'Oh, Pete, I know. But you can blame me. After all, I am older than you . . .'

'Three weeks.'

'. . . and you weren't left in charge of me, or Tony either for that matter. I was. Anyway, we're not doing anything that desperate. Plenty of kids camp out on their own in the summer holidays.'

'All right, all right,' said Pete. 'It's not what you're up to that bothers me, it's what I'm going to have to say. I suppose if I get away with it tonight the best thing is for me to disappear all tomorrow and everyone can think we've gone on a picnic. It'll probably still be pouring with rain. How are you getting home from Pontargwy? I suppose my bike's sitting out in the rain somewhere?'

'It's right under the trees,' said Ruth, guiltily. 'I'll really clean it up for you afterwards, promise.'

'It's not the first time it's got wet,' Pete admitted. 'Tell you one thing, though. There's a long-distance coach tomorrow, runs right up to North Wales somewhere. It comes from Newport right through to Aberafon. That'd be a lot nearer for you than Pontargwy. Gets in about six. If I've got to lose myself all day I'll walk up and collect the bike and cycle down to Aberafon and meet you off the bus there.'

Pete sounded happier now he had thought of a way of getting himself into the scheme for tomorrow, and away from the kindly curiosity of friends and relations.

'That'd be great,' said Ruth. 'Hang on, Tony wants to talk to you.'

She put Tony on to the line, because he was agitating to speak to Pete, but also to give herself time to think. Something did occur to her, and apparently Pete had further thoughts, too, because Tony was saying, 'Wait a sec, I'll ask her.'

'He wants to know where we're spending the night. I've told him it's in some old church,' he said, and Ruth took back the receiver.

'Pete?'

'You'd better tell me exactly where you are, in case Uncle Sam finds out about you, and goes chasing off to get you. If I do know, it won't look so bad, and if he's going to look for you anyway, the easier you are to find the better.'

'It's three miles this side of Pontargwy,' said Ruth. 'There's a sort of lay-by opposite a gas – a petrol station, and the church is in the lay-by. It's called Llan-santffraed – there's an old signpost pointing to it.'

'Hey, there is Uncle Sam, just going down the road. He's pulling in by his place. He'll probably be over to us directly.'

'Then you'd better go. Listen, Pete, we don't want to hang around looking for each other if things go wrong, tomorrow. If we're not on the bus at Aberafon, or if you can't make it, you go straight home, or we will.'

'Right. Damn, Uncle Sam's going straight over to our place, without going into his house at all. I must go. What the hell am I going to say?'

Tony, trying hard to listen, must have heard that bit, for while Ruth looked blank, he seized the phone and said, 'Tell him Ruth's in the woods bringing me back from Old Mossy.'

'Fine. 'Bye.'

' 'Bye,' said Ruth, wresting the phone back from Tony, but it had gone dead.

'I wonder why Uncle Sam was in such a hurry to see us,' she said. 'I wish I could ring Pete back and find out.'

'Forget it,' said Tony. 'I'm having sausage and baked beans on toast; what are you having?'

'We mustn't spend more than we have to,' said Ruth.

'Why not? We've got heaps of money, specially if we're sleeping for free.' They ran across the rain-swept forecourt and into the café.

'It's not really our money, and there's not going to be any more where that came from.'

Tony paused, on his way to the counter. 'Do you mean we're going to be really poor now Dad's dead?'

'I think we may, rather. But I don't honestly know, and anyway don't worry too much about that now. We've got to eat, and, as you say, we're not spending anything on sleeping out.'

'Okay by me.' Tony looked very young and wet as he stood by the counter, and the lady behind it was disposed to mother him.

'My, you have been caught in the rain,' she said. 'What can I get for you, love?'

They gave their orders and sat down at a small table in the window. Three lorry-drivers were sitting round another one, but otherwise the place was empty. Tony, who was facing them, gave Ruth a kick under the table.

'Shall I ask him if he's got a girl-friend in Llanwern?' he whispered.

Ruth glanced round and saw that one of them was the man who had monopolized the telephone for so long.

'Don't you dare,' she muttered.

At that moment one of the other men got up and walked over to the counter to pay for his meal. The lady had disappeared into the room behind, presumably to cook the sausage and beans, but she returned as the man stood tapping a coin on the counter. He bought a packet of chewing-gum and two ham sandwiches – 'for the journey' – at the same time as paying for the meal, and went out to his lorry.

'That's not a bad idea,' said Ruth. 'We'll buy some sandwiches for our breakfast.'

'Can't we come in here and have a proper breakfast?' said Tony.

The lady came over to them with a plate of bread and butter and two bottles of lemonade. 'The beans won't be a moment,' she said, and stood companionably alongside them. 'You on holiday in these parts?'

'Yes,' said Ruth.

'Camping, are you?'

'Yes.'

'Pity the weather's gone so poor. Still, the forecast's good for tomorrow. Staying long?'

'No, only till tomorrow.'

'Family holiday, is it? Gone out for a bit of a look-round on your own this evening, and got caught in the rain, is that it?'

'Yes,' said Ruth.

'We've walked miles,' said Tony, feelingly.

'Then I'd better get your meal quick, or it'll be dark before you get back, and your parents will be wondering what's happened to you. Should be ready now.' And she disappeared into the kitchen.

'That's why we can't come in here again tomorrow morning,' Ruth whispered hastily to Tony. 'It would look suspicious.'

'I guess it would.'

'Tony, that bread and butter's to eat with your dinner, not now.'

'Well, I'm hungry. Have some yourself.' He put a dollop of

159

ketchup on one slice and laid another on top to make a sandwich, squishing the two together so that the ketchup spread out.

'Tony, don't be disgusting.'

'It's good. Nobody's looking.'

Ruth was not so keen on ketchup, but she took care to keep up with Tony slice for slice with the bread, and when the lady returned with the hot meal, the plate was empty.

'There's someone here that's hungry,' she said, putting a friendly hand on Tony's head. 'Shall I cut you some more bread and butter, love?'

'Yes, please,' said Tony quickly before Ruth had time to be conventional and grown-up about it. 'Well, she did ask,' he added defensively, after the lady had gone out to get it. 'And it doesn't cost much, does it? We have to fill up on something before night. Can we afford ice-cream?'

'I don't suppose they have them,' said Ruth, but Tony had seen the advertisement outside on the forecourt.

So they had ice-creams, too, and when they stocked up with sandwiches and chocolate biscuits at the counter afterwards, Ruth felt impelled to mutter something about them being for the rest of the family back at camp.

'What did you say that for?' asked Tony as they left the café. 'You didn't have to, and it isn't even true.'

'It looked awfully greedy if it was just for us, after all we'd eaten.'

'So what?' said Tony. 'Girls!' he added acutely. 'They eat just as much as boys, it's only they pretend not to.'

The light was already beginning to fade as they left the café and crossed the road. They went back the way Ruth had come, because Tony said he hadn't been that way. The shaggy little churchyard was deep in the shadows beneath the encircling forest, and the church itself looked darker still. The approach was conveniently screened, and Ruth and Tony walked up the weedy path without much fear of being observed. Ruth twisted the heavy handle-ring, but the door only creaked open when she gave it a good shove with her shoulder.

'Gee, it's dark!' said Tony. 'Is there a light switch somewhere?'

'Can't feel one,' whispered Ruth, though there was no need for quiet. 'We'll soon get used to it.'

'It doesn't feel very warm,' Tony remarked. It certainly struck chill after the café, and there was a dank, musty smell everywhere. 'Where are we going to sleep?'

'The pews would be warmer than the floor, I should think,' said Ruth, 'but they're awfully narrow.'

'Between the pews? We could sleep side by side then, if one of us slept under the pew.'

'It doesn't look very cosy.'

'Well, find somewhere that does.'

They set about exploring the little church thoroughly. It did not take them very long. A door at the side of the chancel led into a tiny vestry; otherwise the church was simply a rectangle, the lower two-thirds filled with pews, the remainder raised a couple of steps and taken up with the altar and some choirstalls. A harmonica filled the space below the steps on one side, and the pulpit the other. The aisle that ran straight up the centre offered the roomiest accommodation for two children to stretch themselves out side by side, but it was tiled throughout and looked singularly hard and cold and was also, if anyone should come unexpectedly into the church, completely exposed.

'How about the altar?' said Tony.

'Oh, no,' Ruth replied, shocked.

'Do you think God would mind?'

'No, perhaps he wouldn't, but I guess the vicar would.'

'I know. We'll make a bed of kneelers. Let's collect them all together and see how many they make.'

'I wonder if there's anything we could wrap around us,' said Ruth, wishing they were in a nice hay-filled barn, rats and all. While Tony busied himself shunting hassocks up the aisle, she went exploring in the vestry, and found three decaying cassocks hanging up behind a ragged green baize curtain. She took them down, and then decided to unhook the curtain as well. They were all impregnated with the musty smell, but that could not be helped. Going back into the church, she could see Tony busy with his kneelers by the pulpit.

'Look,' he said. 'The front pew is just flat, like this; it hasn't got a seat in front of it. We can put the kneelers against it like so, and there's room for us both between it and the pulpit, and that bit of the pew should help stop the kneelers coming apart in the middle.'

'Good,' said Ruth. 'And I've got some things to wrap up in. What's that?' For something had flittered across the slim oval of light formed by one of the windows.

'What's what?'

'Oh, nothing.' But she knew it must have been a bat. Presumably it was still flying around above her head, only she couldn't see it unless it crossed the window again, for the interior was getting very dark indeed now. 'I'm not sure, Tony, it wouldn't be better to sleep between and under the pew, like you suggested first. I think it would be warmer than out here.'

'You can't,' said Tony. 'I've been looking. There's a sort of solid bit comes down under the middle of each one, and cuts the space in half. You'd be too tall to get in, and I don't want to. I'd feel weird poked in under there.'

Ruth looked at the nearest window. The light was fading fast and the rain was pattering against the stained glass. It was too late and too wet to suggest going anywhere else now. The church it must be, bats and all.

The kneelers were not a great success. They arranged them in a broad rectangle, covered them with one cassock, and then lay down on them with the curtain and the other cassocks on top of them. The strain of lying still enough not to disturb the kneelers made them tense and most unsleepy; after a bit Tony began to wriggle, and the kneelers all came apart and left parts of both of them suspended over holes. In any case, there were not enough to accommodate Ruth's feet, which stuck out over the end.

'I think it would be better without them,' Tony admitted eventually, and Ruth agreed. They pushed them outwards to form a barricade against the draught, and lay down again.

Now they only had one worn damp cassock beneath them, and the tiled floor was very hard and very cold.

'We'd be better with the curtain underneath us and the cassocks all on top,' said Ruth after quarter of an hour.

Tony sat up. 'It's absolutely pitch dark,' he said. 'I ... I don't like it.'

It really was dark, with that depth of blackness that presses on the eyes. Not a glimmer seemed to come now through the stained-glass windows, discoloured and cobwebby and shaded by the fir trees.

'I wonder what the time is,' said Ruth. 'I wish I'd thought to bring a torch.'

'There must be some light-switches somewhere in this church,' said Tony. 'Can't you find them?'

'The trouble is if anyone sees a light shining from here they'll come and investigate.'

'Nobody would, surely. The church is right out of sight from the main road and that café.'

'I've got it,' said Ruth. 'Candles. There's always candles in churches. They wouldn't show much.'

'What are you going to light them with?'

'Oh, damnation. Well, there might be matches somewhere, too.'

'I wish you'd do something to find us some sort of light. Anything would be better than this dark, dark, darkness.'

'All right, then.' Ruth spoke gently, for she knew that Tony was close to panic. 'Only it will take some time to creep all round in the dark by feel. Do you want to come with me?'

'No. Yes, yes I do,' he said quickly as Ruth began to move away. She groped for his hand, and together they crept down the aisle towards the door. Once Ruth heard a soft fluttering, and a breath of air stirred across her forehead. She gulped, and involuntarily tried to snatch her hand from Tony's grasp.

'Don't leave go,' said Tony, 'please.'

'I could feel my way better from pew to pew if I had two hands,' said Ruth. 'You hang on to my anorak.' But she used her spare hand first to put her hood up.

'What are you doing?' said Tony. 'Come on.'

'Coming. I'm on the last pew, I think. Yes. We should be at the door directly. Yes, here it is.'

She ran her hand up and down the rough wall alongside the door, feeling for a panel of switches, but found nothing.

'Try the other side of the door,' said Tony.

They worked their way across the broad heavy door, and patted up and down the wall on the far side.

'It's no good,' Ruth was just about to say, when she felt what she was looking for – a square board with about six switches plugged into it. The only trouble was that all the switches were already down.

'Perhaps they work upside-down,' said Tony hopefully, and Ruth switched them all up, but nothing happened.

'They just don't work at all,' she said. It did not occur to either of them that they might find a master switch in the vestry or wherever the main fuse was.

'Let's look for matches then,' said Tony.

'Feel for, more like,' said Ruth. 'But that would be pretty hopeless, and even if we did find any they'd probably be damp. If we just went back to bed and you lay down and shut your eyes, you wouldn't know whether it was dark or not.'

'I wouldn't mind it being dark so much if I could just have a light for a moment,' said Tony. 'Just to remind me where everything is. It's the not knowing where you are that's frightening.'

It's the not knowing where the bats are, thought Ruth, but she did not say anything. They were working their way back up towards the pulpit by now.

'There might be matches in that little room where the vicar changes,' said Tony.

'The vestry. I didn't see any when I was in there, but I wasn't looking specially, and it was beginning to get pretty dark then. We'll go up there and have a look if you like.'

They padded laboriously up to the vestry, and felt all around the table and shelves in there. Ruth did not enjoy it much; there was always the feeling you did not quite know what you were going to put your hand on next. For one exhilarating moment, she thought she had triumphed. Her fingers closed over a box that was evidently a matchbox, that rattled when she shook it. But when she opened it, the box was half-full of drawing-pins.

Tony suddenly yawned. 'Come on,' he said. 'I'm getting sleepy.'

'Fine by me,' said Ruth, a little shortly, because she would much prefer to be lying still in the dark than prowling around the bat-infested building. 'I thought you were too scared to sleep in the dark?'

'I've gotten used to it,' said Tony. Moving around the church hand-in-hand with Ruth had given him a sense of direction and a feeling of familiarity with his surroundings, and the dark was less oppressive. He began to lead the way back down the chancel. 'I wish we could find our way around by squeaking to ourselves, like the bats,' he remarked.

'Bats?' said Ruth. She had heard a few faint squeaks, but had hoped they would escape Tony's attention.

'Yes. Haven't you heard them? One nearly flew into my face just now.'

'Yes,' said Ruth. 'I was hoping you hadn't heard them.'

'I'm not afraid of *bats*,' said Tony. 'They're only mice with wings. There's always bats in churches.'

'Yes, but they swoop about so,' said Ruth.

'They'll never bash into you, though,' said Tony knowledge-ably. 'They hear their own echo bouncing off things, and then they know where they are. You scared they'll get all tangled up in your hair?'

'Rather,' said Ruth humbly.

'That's just an old wives' tale. I'll bet your hair echoes like anything. Shall I go in front if you're scared?'

'I don't see that makes much difference,' said Ruth ungraciously, 'but you can if you like.'

'Clear off, bats. We're coming. Hey, is this the organ thing? Mightn't there be a box of matches there?'

They felt all over it, and lifted up the lid and felt along the silent keys, but found nothing.

'If that's the organ, then the pulpit's straight across,' said Ruth.

'Why don't we sleep in the pulpit?' said Tony. 'We could fill it with kneelers, and then they wouldn't be able to fall apart.'

'We wouldn't have room to stretch out, not me, anyway.'

'I think there's a sort of platform where the steps go up. You could stick your legs out there. So could I, come to that, if I needed to.'

'It's worth a try. Let's see what it feels like before we put all the kneelers up there.'

They fumbled their way up the steps and lay down. It gave them a pleasant enclosed feeling. Tony chose to curl up in the space available, but Ruth found she did need the extra length of the top step. She climbed down again and passed the kneelers up to Tony who stacked them systematically all over the floor space of the pulpit. At first she put them into his hands one by one round by the entrance, but after a bit she just dropped them in over the top.

As she passed the fourth one over in this way, she caught something balanced on the top near the wall, and it fell into the pulpit with a rattle. It sounded unmistakably like a match-box.

'Timber!' said Tony. He patted around, and soon retrieved it.

'Bet they won't light,' said Ruth. Tony struck three in succession, and they all disintegrated without a spark. 'You try,' he said.

Ruth tried a couple in the same way without success, and then ran her finger over the tiles on the floor till she identified a line of rough mortar between two tiles. She struck the next match along this, and it sputtered into life but died before she could do anything with it.

'We need something to light from it straightaway,' she said. 'A spill or something.'

'Hang on, I've got some paper here that will make a spill.' Tony passed a roughly rolled-up piece of paper to her, and she twisted it carefully into shape before the next attempt. This time she managed to capture the weak flame before it went out, and watched it flare up at the end of the paper.

'Quick!' she said. 'A candle. Get one from the altar.'

'Here!' said Tony. 'There's one here, on the pulpit. Look!'

There they were, two candles in old brass brackets, put there years ago so that the preacher could read his notes, and never replaced when electricity was installed.

Ruth lit them both, and the clear warm glow dispelled the blackness. They looked at each other's faces across the flame, Tony up in the pulpit, Ruth down below, and smiled. The bleak edges of their adventure dissolved away.

'You'd better blow that paper out, or it'll burn your fingers,' said Tony, and Ruth realized the spill was still alight. It was quite difficult to blow out, and in the effort several charred flakes fluttered to the ground. She suddenly looked at the paper more closely, and began to unroll it.

'Why!' she said. 'Tony! This is your picture.'

'I know,' he said. 'It wasn't any good anyway. It got all crumpled up in my pocket. I'd lost the second prize certificate somewhere, which is the only thing I really wanted to show Patsy. The picture wasn't all that good. I can drew her another one any day.'

'But I've got your certificate!' said Ruth. 'It's in my anorak pocket. I found it at the cross-roads in the forest.'

'You haven't really, have you?' asked Tony, and Ruth fished it out of her pocket and handed it over. It was a bit crumpled, but that did not matter. 'Did you know I'd won it?'

'Only when Pete told me. You never said.'

'You never asked.'

'I thought, as you hadn't said anything, you hadn't won anything, so I'd better not ask.'

'Oh,' said Tony. 'I thought you had just forgotten about it.'

Ruth changed the subject. 'How do those hassocks look in there?'

'Hassocks?'

'Kneelers. You know.'

'I thought those were the long black things that smell like toadstools.'

'Those are cassocks.'

'Have you got any more hassocks then?'

'Four. No, five. No, six.'

'Make up your mind.'

'Well, the candlelight doesn't reach very far, and half of them are all in the shadows.'

'Anyway, there's only room for three more, but we could put some out on the steps for your toes.'

When completed, the hassock-lined pulpit looked like some cosy nest; they discovered there were two breeds, one thick and one thin, so they used the thin ones for pillows, and to wedge beside their hips. Now that the hassocks needed no firmer anchorage, they could use all the available coverings to put over themselves.

Tony snuggled down in the front curve of the pulpit, wrapped in one of the cassocks. Ruth fiddled around for a while, blowing out one of the candles and arranging the old curtain and the two remaining cassocks to best advantage. Then she turned sideways and prepared to settle down, but just at that moment, although she was not looking at it, a flickering shadow swooped between her and the candle.

Bats! she thought, and stared fixedly at the flame, which bowed and smoked as though a draught had just hit it.

She did not have long to wait to be sure of it. First one bat fluttered low over the candle, then another; then there seemed an endless succession as they swooped in from the blackness, weaving in and out of each other's trails, squeaking in miniscule voices.

A big moth blundered into the flame, and Ruth realized that the light was attracting scores of flying creatures, mosquitos and daddy-long-legs and innumerable flies and moths. That must be what the bats are after, she thought. So if I blow the candle out, not only will I not *see* the bats, they won't be there. She pondered for a while on whether it was better to see bats, or just guess at them.

'Tony?' she said inquiringly. There was no reply. She leaned over him, astonished that he could have dropped to sleep so quickly, but he had.

I guess once he had some light he could relax, she thought. And I'm sure I could relax better without it. She made sure she had the matches safe, and scrambled nervously to her feet. She licked her fingers and pinched the flame out, at arm's length so as to avoid putting her head too close to the main bat-way.

Sleep did not come at once, though. For a while she lay straining her ears for the swish of leather wings or the staccato squeaks, but all was quiet. Then a mosquito started droning in her ear. She slapped at it, but without success. She pulled the curtain over her head, but it was tickly and stuffy. She began to worry about what Uncle Sam had wanted, about what it would be like waking up in the grey dawn with a long day to plan ahead, and only a few sandwiches in a cheerless church to see them on their way. Oh dear, she thought. I shall never sleep. And slept.

Chapter 10

SHE was woken by the sound of a heavy door closing. '*Closing?*' her half-wakened mind queried. She opened her eyes, but all was perfectly dark and in any case the only part of the church she could have seen was the strip opposite the pulpit entrance, immediately beyond her own toes.

The realization that someone or something had *closed* the door was, if anything, more frightening than if she had heard it opening. Either the person or thing had gone, having been inside, shutting the door behind them (locking it, too?) or they had just come in, and were somewhere in the church now, moving purposefully and silently towards the pulpit.

It was scarcely conceivable that Tony should have got up and gone out into the churchyard by himself, taken short in the night, without waking her for company, still less that he would have shut the door behind him, but she put her hand surreptitiously out to where he should be, and at once encountered his sleeping body.

Ruth became acutely conscious, in her terror, of her feet dangling over the edge of the pulpit steps. She had taken off her wet gym shoes before lying down, and in her sleep had kicked the cassock off her feet; they stuck out naked and unprotected, while she herself, enclosed within the pulpit, could see nothing.

The silence continued long enough for Ruth to begin to try and persuade herself that she had dreamt the sound, when it was broken by a faint rustling noise. Then a small light shone.

Ruth could not see the beam, but only a dim reflection of it on the roof above her head. Then the shaft passed the pulpit entrance, shining straight up the aisle. In the next instant, it switched to the side, and there were her two feet, white and glaring in the torchlight. She snatched them to her, sitting up tight against the further wall.

'Ruth? It's me, Pete.'

'Ooh!' The cry came out half gasp, half sob. She flung the coverings over on to Tony, and almost fell down the steps. 'Pete, you scared me!'

'I'm sorry. I didn't put the light on straightaway for fear of waking you and frightening you.'

'You frightened me anyway.' She realized she was clutching at his jacket, and let go, rather shamefaced.

'Sorry,' he said again. 'Where's Tony?'

'Here.' She took his torch from him, and pointed out the sleeping figure. 'What are you doing here? Why have you come? How did you get here?'

'I'll tell you. But don't let's wake Tony. Let's go and sit at the back of the church. I've got a couple of blankets down by the door, and a flask. Like a cup of coffee? You're shivering.'

'I'll put my shoes on.' The damp plimsolls were not very comforting, but they were better than cold tiles under bare feet.

'Pete, however did you bring all these things? How did you get here?'

'On a horse.'

'A *horse*?'

'Yeah, well, you'd pinched my bicycle.'

'Sorry. But why have you come?'

'I'll tell you when we're settled.' Pete retrieved the blankets, tied up with string into a neat roll with the flask inside. They sat on the back pew well swathed in blankets, and only when Pete had poured out a cup of coffee did he begin to talk.

'Sorry I've only got one cup, and we'd better have half each because we may want the rest later.'

'Pete, I don't really want any. We had a real good supper at that café after I called you. I'll just have a mouthful to warm me up. Tell me why you've come.'

'You know Uncle Sam was coming straight over to our place when you rang?'

'Yes.'

'He came to say he'd swopped duties for Thursday and Friday – that's tomorrow – no, today.' He looked at his watch. It was twelve-thirty. 'And instead of going to Newport on Friday he's going on Thursday. They'd rung up from the hospital to say could Patsy come home because she was fine and they needed the bed, so then he rang Mum and fixed that he'll collect Patsy about eleven o'clock, and go on with her to Bristol to see Auntie Sybil, who's doing fine after the operation, by the way – he told me that, too – and come home in the evening bringing Mum with him. And he said he'd take Tony as well as you, because your mother wanted to see him so badly.'

'So we've got to get back straightaway if he's not to find out?'

'That's it.'

'All that trouble to get Tony to see Patsy, and now he might miss the chance of seeing either of them; Pete, what happens if we don't get back, and Uncle Sam finds the house empty?'

Pete had turned the torch off, and was sipping coffee in the dark. Ruth could hear the grin in his voice when he answered. 'Don't laugh,' he said. 'I left a note.'

'Can it be done?'

'Can what be done?'

'Can we get home before they discover?'

'It took me four hours to get here, and that meant leading Betty all along the green road, because it was pitch dark, but I thought it would be quicker than riding all around, which would look odd, too, and anyway I reckoned she'd be too exhausted to get home again if I did that. I thought of leaving her up by the bike, but I was scared she'd break loose if I tied her up. It shouldn't take longer going back, because it's about the same up and down either way, and we'll have the bike as well, and two of us can ride Betty.'

'You must be exhausted.'

'Yeah, well, I reckoned I could have a bit of a kip before starting back. How much sleep have you had, anyway?'

'I don't know. It was about half-past eight when we got here, I suppose, after the meal at the café. Then we fiddled about trying to find some sort of light, and getting ourselves comfortable. I should think Tony went off about half-past nine, and me about an hour later. It wasn't really late, because once we were in here and it was dark, there wasn't anything else to do.'

'That means you've had about two hours, and Tony three, and I haven't had any.'

'Tony must have slept for two or three hours in the forest.'

'Good, because he's the one most likely to hold us back.'

Ruth felt an irrational urge to defend Tony, but she let it pass.

'The thing is,' Pete went on, 'we'll have to start before it gets light, which is a pity, because it's slow going through that track in the dark, and we shall only have one torch between the three of us. That's why I've switched it off now, because it's getting rather dim already.'

'If you want a light now I can light a candle. That's what we did. I've got some matches.' She gave the box in her pocket a rattle.

'No need. We might wake Tony, and the more sleep he gets the better. Let's work backwards. Uncle Sam is calling for us at nine. That means we ought to get back by eight, and the last bit's going to be tricky in case we're seen.'

'We ought to leave by four at the latest then.'

'That's right. I wonder when it starts getting light?'

'It was beginning when I came down this morning to get Uncle Jack his breakfast – that was about five.'

'Actually it's never *really* dark outside when you're used to

173

it. I could see the sky between the trees, just, coming down the track, but the trouble is you can't see where you're going. I had the dickens of a job getting Betty to start down the top bit, which is all rocks and steep – you remember – and lower down we kept getting stuck in the brambles.'

'Did you know the green road?'

'Yes. I've been down it from the top end with Tom when we've been out on a bicycle ride, but I've never walked right through and out at the bottom. I very nearly missed the church – I did miss it in fact, but when I came out on the main road I knew where I was from what you'd said, so it was easy then.'

There was a sudden commotion in the porch, heavy footsteps and a blowing noise.

'What's that?' whispered Ruth nervously.

Pete laughed. 'It's only Betty. I turned her loose in the churchyard. I expect she's come in for a bit of shelter. I hope she behaves herself in the porch. We're taking a bit of a liberty with this church, aren't we?'

'We'd better put something in the box before we go,' said Ruth. 'Who's Betty, and where did you get her? Tygwyn? I hope she's not one of the rodeo ponies if you expect me to ride her, or Tony either for that matter.'

'Anyone could ride old Betty. That's why I took her – that and because she's easy to catch. Luckily she was down in the trees by the stream. I had more of a job getting the saddle and that than I had getting Betty. Luckily they were all having supper at Tygwyn, so I was able to slip into the stable and get the stuff without being seen. I hope they don't miss it before tomorrow – or Betty, come to that, but I don't think they'll miss her. She's in the field behind our place at the moment, and spends a lot of her time under the trees where they can't see her. They'll only notice if someone wants to ride her, and they're not likely to do that before eight o'clock tomorrow morning.'

174

'They'll find her pretty tired whatever time they want her tomorrow.'

'Poor old Betty. But it's not likely anyone'll be needing her. She's the one they mostly use for shepherding, because she's quiet and sensible, but there's not a lot of shepherding to be done at this time of year. It's not the lambing season, and the shearing and dipping's done. You sure you don't want any more coffee?'

'No, keep it till we go. I've got some sandwiches for then, too, from the café. Would you like one now?'

'No, I've been eating on the way. I just want to sleep now. Where do you recommend?'

'Tony and I were both in the pulpit, and we've put all the hassocks in there for a mattress. I think there's room for you, too.'

Pete considered a moment, weighing up a boyish regard for his dignity against the call of comfort and warmth.

'Are you sure?' he asked. He switched on his torch and they surveyed the pulpit with Tony curled up in one corner of it.

Ruth rolled herself up in a blanket and lay down close to Tony, to make the other half of the pulpit look like a private establishment.

'There you are,' she said. 'Take it or leave it.'

'I'll take it,' said Pete. As he humped himself in the other blanket and Ruth disposed the old curtain over the three of them, he added unexpectedly, 'There's always a first time to share a bed with a girl.'

'Huh,' said Ruth, and lay down with her back to him. A moment later, though, she turned her head. 'Pete,' she said, 'how are we going to wake up in time?'

But Pete had gone to sleep.

Ruth decided she had better stay awake for the rest of the night; but it was warm now, with an extra body and two extra blankets, and since Pete's arrival, and the change of plan, there was little to worry about. At least, nothing serious. Tony was safe, and so were she and Pete; Patsy was coming out of hospital, and her mother was well on the way to recovery. The worst that could happen to them was that their escapade would be discovered, and thinking about it Ruth realized that the most dangerous moment had passed. If Uncle Sam was going to return to their house at all, it was likely to have been later on in the evening, to check up on whether she and Tony had come home safely from Old Mossy's, if that was what Pete had told their uncle. If he had done so, and found Pete gone, too, and Pete's note left out for him, he would have been here by now, for it was only half an hour's run in the car.

Even the bats seemed to have gone back to bed. Sleep swept over her in waves; three or four times she pushed them away, but the next time she sank blissfully into them.

She was woken by Tony, talking in his sleep. 'Get off,' he was saying. 'You're squashing me. Get off, you old horse, get off.' He kicked at her.

'I'm not a horse,' said Ruth, with the absurd indignation of someone roused prematurely from sleep.

'Eh? Oh.' Tony began to surface. He thrashed about a bit, then spoke with sudden urgency. 'Hi, Ruth, do you remember where we are? Wake up, Ruth.'

'I am awake,' she said drowsily, 'so stop kicking. Hi, golly, yes I am awake, and we've got to go.'

'Go? Now?' Horses' hooves clonked in the tiled porch. 'That sounds like a horse. That's it, I knew it was a horse, I heard it in my sleep. I dreamt a horse was sitting on top of me and – hey, Ruth, where'd you get that from?' Ruth had groped for Pete's torch, lying between them, and switched it on.

'I can see why you felt squashed,' said Ruth, for she had rolled over in her sleep and pinned her brother tight against the wall. 'But it's a good thing if it woke you up, because we've got to get up.' She was looking at her watch; it said four-fifteen.

'Why? Hey, who's that?' He had caught sight of the rolled-up bundle that was Pete.

'It's Pete. He came in the night. Ssh, now, and I'll explain quickly, because we've got to get going.'

She got up and lit the two candles as she talked, and told Tony to wake Pete up. She went on answering Tony's questions as she hung the cassocks and the curtain back up in the vestry, combed her hair, and tried to pull her anorak and trousers into some sort of presentable shape. They had dried off from the worst of the rain in the warmth of the café, but it had still been drizzling when they ran across to the church, and although their clothes had never been wet through, the surface moisture and the dankness of the cassocks left them now feeling crumpled and clammy.

When Pete came to, they all sat round and ate the sandwiches and drank the hot coffee, which made them feel much better. Afterwards, Ruth insisted that they put the kneelers back in the pews. When she went to see what had happened to Tony, who had gone to ground at the back of the church with the torch, she found him busily writing his name in the visitor's book.

'Don't do that, stupid,' she cried. 'We don't want anyone to know we've been here.'

'Nobody will look, unless they know anyway,' said Tony. 'And it will be neat to come back years later and see our names here.'

'Oh, come on,' said Pete, who had been tying up the blankets. 'Let's all sign.' So they did, and then Pete blew out the candles.

'Thanks, God,' said Tony, as they turned to go.

There was no problem about catching Betty in the dark. They opened the church door and she walked in.

She was large and brown and friendly, not at all like the skittering creatures in the rodeo ring. More like a teddy-bear than a horse, thought Ruth, who had never had much to do with horses, and perpetually quelled an urge to be afraid of them.

'Hullo, Betty,' said Tony. 'You know me, don't you?'

'Does she?' asked Ruth, surprised.

'Of course,' said Tony. 'I've often talked to her when I go through the field to Tygwyn. Haven't you?'

Ruth had to admit she had never really noticed Betty.

'You must know her. She's bigger than Shandy, and much tamer, and they're the only ones that are always there, aren't they, Pete?'

'Who's Shandy?'

'That's the little one Tom was riding in the morning at the Show, you know, when he was bringing the other ponies in. Can I ride first?'

'You can ride all the way if you want to, because old Betty won't mind taking two at a time, specially if one is small,' said Pete. He was fumbling at the girths in the dark.

'Give us the torch,' said Tony, taking it from Ruth's hand and directing it much more knowledgeably where Pete was trying to do up the buckles.

Ruth walked out into the open and looked at the sky. The rain had stopped, and the sky was quite light, as though there was a moon shining somewhere behind the clouds. She moved further away from the church, and could then see that there was indeed a pale patch in the clouds, low over the hills to the west, and as she watched the clouds drifted away, and the moon shone through, bright and clear. 'Look!' she called softly. 'Moonlight! We shan't have to worry about the dark.'

The tilted gravestones cast long dark shadows on the rough grass. The church, between her and the moon, crouched black beneath the firs that speared the sky, except for one place where the hill rose sheer enough and steep enough to be visible over the tops of the trees. That must be the bluff I stood on, thought Ruth. Behind her, the low churchyard wall was moonwashed bright as day, but far more mysterious. The ivy and the tufts of hair-stemmed tiny ferns, the lichens on the side, and the moss along the coping, interspersed with thin grasses and hare-bells, were all etched in intricate detail, yet drained of any colour save silver and grey and black.

The silence was beautiful, underlined, not masked, by the subdued jangle of bit and bridle and the clop of hooves in the porch. Ruth could hear old Betty working the bit around in her mouth till it sat comfortably, and the shiny stiff sound of Pete's oilskin jacket, an old one of his father's with the firm's name stencilled on the back. She could see the letters clearly when the moonlight fell upon them, yet the oilskin, which she knew to be a bright yellow, looked shadow-grey.

When Pete led Betty out, she could see Tony was already in the saddle. He had scarcely ever been on a horse, to Ruth's knowledge, but had mounted now without fuss or fear, and sat there in perfect confidence. Hedgehogs, bats, horses, she thought. She remembered how often he had asked for a pet in their New York apartment, and been told it was impossible. Ruth had never thought about it as being a *real* need, just something to whine about, like wanting Mommy whenever things went wrong. If they came to live here, near Pete's family, Tony could have a pet.

'Want a leg up?' asked Pete.

Ruth looked at the placid animal. Betty smelt comfortably earthy in the fey moonlit churchyard.

'You forget,' she said, 'neither of us know how to ride. You get up with Tony; I'll have my turn later on if I have to.'

'Just as you like,' said Pete, and swung up into the saddle behind Tony.

'Can I hold the reins?' asked Tony.

'Wait till we get on the forest track, then you can take them,' said Pete.

They scrunched along the gravel path, brushed through the lych-gate and clopped up the quiet road. A single heavy lorry roared by above the blackthorn thicket. Betty turned into the old path readily enough; she must have realized they were going home.

The forest track was five miles long. After two miles they came to the crossway where Ruth had picked up the prize certificate, and she was glad enough to swop places with Pete. Tony got down, too, saying he would like to walk for a change, but he soon found it heavy going, and got back up again. The moon had set now, hastened by the fact that they were working their way further into the lee of the mountainside, but a grey light was spreading over the plain behind them. The general layout of the land was easy to see so far as the trees allowed it, but not the detail of the ground beneath their feet.

Old Betty plodded along, head nodding, the strong shoulder muscles taking the strain of the upwards incline, and if now and again one foot slipped on an unexpected stone or sunk in unseen mud, it did not seem to bother her. Ruth realized it made little difference whether she or Tony held the reins. Old Betty regarded Pete as her master whether he was riding her or not, and she would have gone with him whatever the other two did.

At first he went ahead and she followed, her nose to his shoulder, but when they came to the thick brambles and bracken, and Betty seemed able to pick her way through the gloom along the tracks she had made earlier, Pete found it easier to follow in her footsteps. Then she was inclined to lag, waiting for him to get in front again, but Pete made encouraging noises from behind so that Betty knew he was still close to her and she was content to accept their altered position.

As the ground got steeper, and first the brambles and then the thinning patches of bracken fell away behind them, Ruth began to feel it was unfair on the patient horse to expect her to go on carrying two people, and she slid off. In any case, it was difficult to stay in the saddle, with Tony slipping back against her, for someone as unaccustomed to riding as she.

Colour was creeping into the landscape. The whin and grasses took on a soft jade tinge that distingushed them from the brown bog grasses, and the purple heather patches began to stand out. The trees, that endless wall on either side of their mountain corridor, changed from black to dark green, and the trunks stood out paler against the still unfathomable darkness of the forest underworld. Suddenly their own shadows appeared, wavering ghosts on the hillside ahead of them, and looking back, they saw the bright ball of the sun edging up over the distant plain.

'Hooray!' said Tony. 'Now perhaps it will get warmer.'

'Are you cold?' asked Ruth in surprise, for though the dawn air had been distinctly chill, they had climbed the best part of a thousand feet. Tony, however, had been riding nearly all the way. 'Get off, and run up the hill. That should warm you.'

'But I like it here,' said Tony. He was loth to leave the warmth of the horse, although, like a cooling bath, he would be colder in the long run if he stayed there.

'You'd better get off anyway,' said Pete. 'This last half-mile is really steep, and old Betty will just have to scramble up as best she can.'

It was a scramble for all of them, and Pete was beginning to get worried about the time, so he did not let them rest. By the time they got to the main road at the top, none of them were complaining of cold. The sun was well up, and shining full upon the slope of the hill, but the plain still lay in shadow.

'Just think,' said Ruth. 'If we were still in the church, the sun wouldn't have risen yet.'

Pete looked at his watch. 'You're right,' he said. 'It's only ten past six now. I thought it was later than it was because of the sunrise, but of course we rose it early, climbing up like this.'

'Do you think we'll be okay? We haven't come nearly half-way.'

Tony groaned, but Pete was optimistic.

'Oh, yes, should be. After all, we've got the bike now, and once we get up on the level, by the signpost, we'll get along much faster.'

'Do you think I'm going to gallop?' asked Ruth, but Tony was all agog to do so.

Pete mounted Betty behind Tony, and Ruth got on the bicycle. It was a hard pull up to the signpost, but even so she was able to keep up with Betty trotting. Pete kept asking her if she wouldn't rather change places with him, but she declined. She felt safer where she was. Tony jiggled and giggled uncontrollably, for even if he had known how to rise in the saddle, his legs were dangling free, because Pete had his feet in the stirrups. At first it was fun, but soon he was begging Pete to slow down to a walk.

'It'll be better when we canter,' said Pete. 'But we'll walk now, to the top of the hill, to give Betty and Ruth a rest, but after that we'll really go.'

From the signpost to the hamlet of Llandewi the road ran pretty level along the crest of the moorland, and a wide band of short turf edged the road on either side. Old Betty lengthened her stride and rocked along at a canter that left Tony breathless and sparkling, while Ruth bowled alongside on the bicycle. It was an exhilarating ride in the early dawn, a ride to remember.

They cantered straight through Llandewi, no doubt to the surprise of that sleeping village, only dropping to a trot to mount the rise on the other side. At the top, where later in the day tourists would picnic, where Ruth had first glimpsed Old Mossy, they stopped and rested, looking down into their own valley. The sun was warm and bright on their backs, and it was hard to realize that for Llanwern the dawn had not broken. The shadows still engulfed the village, nooked on the western side of the moors, and a skein of mist marked out the course of the brook. A buzzard mewed overhead, mobbed by a couple of squawking crows, and from the nearest farm below them, Aberdulais, they could hear the cows mooing as they emerged from the milking-shed and wandered out into the dew-fresh field.

'Please can I have a turn on the bicycle now?' said Tony.

'Now that it's all downhill?' said Ruth.

'If you knew how sore I was ...' Tony rubbed his legs tenderly. 'And bruised. Bumping up and down on this knobbly bit of the saddle. If I can't ride, I'll walk.'

'Actually, it's pretty steep down here,' said Pete. 'You'd fall over the horse's head anyway. It isn't so bad further down.'

'Tell you what,' said Ruth. 'I'll ride the bike down a little way, and then leave it for Tony and start walking, and so on. That way we'll keep up with you.'

'Get ahead, most likely,' said Pete. 'Betty won't go very fast down this top bit.'

Tony was quite glad to have a rest from a saddle of any sort, and while Ruth spun ahead down the hill, he jogged beside Pete as Betty half trotted, half walked, her forefeet splayed out in front of her, her hooves slipping from time to time on the gravel. Ruth had expected Tony to demand first turn on the bicycle, and was relieved he hadn't, because she was afraid he might have tried to take the upper hill too fast, and go hurtling out of control. The hill was a very long one, winding down the side of the mountain through a series of hairpin bends.

She kept the brakes on firmly, and even so the front tyre was inclined to judder on the loose chippings, and by the time she rounded the first sharp bend, she was ready to give her aching fingers a rest from clutching the brakes. She laid the bicycle on the ground above an old stunted hawthorn, bearing the scars of the impact of a car, and she remembered a story Tony had once told her, which he had heard from Gary, about Tom and Pete playing around with the roadside reflectors one night, so that an unsuspecting van ran over the edge. The driver was only saved from disaster by a lucky tree that prevented the van from plunging to the bottom of the ravine. Ruth had not really believed Tony, but now she changed her mind. For someone as seemingly sedate and sensible as Pete, he had done some remarkably daft things in his life, like slipping off to Scotland to see his father when everybody imagined he had gone on the school trip to Germany. And not only Pete, she reflected, thinking about their present escapade.

She walked on down the hill, hearing the now familiar clip-clop of Betty's hooves behind her, and then the whirr of bicycle wheels as Tony sailed down towards her.

'Don't go too fast!' she called, 'and wait for us at the bottom!'

There was no reply, and Ruth wondered whether he had heard the last bit. She hoped he would not cycle boldly through the village, forgetting how odd it would look at that time of day. She was sure nobody had ever seen Tony up and about before eight o'clock in the morning.

Pete and Betty caught her up at that point, and Pete set her mind at rest by assuring her he had impressed on Tony that he was to wait for them by the bridge, and hide below it if he heard anyone coming. 'Hang on a sec,' he said. 'I'm awfully hot in this oilskin, and if anyone does see me and think I've gone for a short ride before breakfast they'll wonder what the heck I'm rigged out like this for.'

The sun was now slanting down the valley, and their elongated shadows marched before them. The roofs of the village, wet from the overnight rain, gleamed among the trees and Uncle Sam's greenhouse winked at them like a lighthouse.

Pete jammed the oilskin under the roll of blankets tied to the back of the saddle.

'Pete,' said Ruth, 'you know when you went off to Scotland. You never really told me why.'

'Didn't I?'

'There's no need, if you don't want to. Only it sounds as dumb as what we're doing now.'

'No reason why not. The brother of a school pal of mine, and another boy, were pinching sweets — and money, too, only I didn't know that till after — and I stopped to talk to Vince — that's my friend — while he was keeping watch. Then, when they were found out, it looked as though I'd been in on it from the start.' He glanced up at Ruth as he fiddled with the saddle. 'I hadn't, honest.'

'I believe you.'

'The Head didn't, though. He said no school trip for me. I felt sore because Mum had killed herself to get the money and all. And I was fed up with Dad always being away, and Mum wouldn't let me go and visit him. His firm has got a contract near here, next, though, so he'll be coming home. You knew that, did you?'

'Yeah,' said Ruth. 'I heard Auntie Mary tell Mom. That's great. About your mother saving up the money, though – it doesn't really make sense, you going off like that, does it?' she added, thoughtfully.

'No,' said Pete. He grinned. 'But it was worth it. I had a great time getting there – that's how I got to know Alan. I'll tell you all about it some time.' He held the stirrup for Ruth to get up. 'I learnt a lot, too. About Dad – and Mum, too, I suppose. Come on. Old Betty can manage the two of us this last mile. You've covered more of the journey under your own steam than any of us.'

'If you trot I'll fall off,' said Ruth, as Pete gave her a leg-up.

'O.K., we won't trot,' said Pete, swinging up behind her. 'We'll gallop.'

'Hey, Pete, don't! Whoa, Betty! Stop it!'

It wasn't really a gallop, for Betty, anxious to get home though she was, had no intention of killing herself with fourteen stone on her back; but she was a sturdy animal, used to carrying Tom's hefty brother Kevin on long shepherding expeditions over the hills, and glad enough to canter the last mile home.

It felt like a gallop to Ruth. 'I shall fall off!' she cried. 'Hold me tight!' She gripped the front of the saddle with one hand and Betty's mane with the other, and hung on for dear life. She would have taken the reins from Pete's easy grasp, and pulled them in, but she dared not loosen her grip with either hand. Pete's right arm held her firm, and she leaned back against him, for fear of falling over the horse's neck, for there was not much room for two of them on the saddle.

'Get your hair out of my mouth!' shouted Pete, laughing and spluttering.

'Then stop her!' she shouted back, and then, at once, 'No, don't. It's tremendous!' for the thrill of the mad ride sparkled through her.

They swung round one corner, but at the next the ground dropped steeply again for a few yards, and Betty skithered unbidden to a walk.

'Oh, Pete,' gasped Ruth, 'that was terrible!' Her bright eyes and flushed cheeks belied her words. 'My poor bottom!'

'You've got a darn sight too much hair,' said Pete, and raising it in an untidy hank with his right hand, he kissed her clumsily on the back of the neck.

Ruth was so taken aback, she sat speechless and motionless.

New York boys were freer with their kisses than Welsh ones of the same age, and Patsy was always getting kissed, casually, as one picks up a cuddly puppy and kisses it. But none of her class-mates had ever offered to kiss Ruth, nor had she ever expected them to. She had always assumed she was going to grow up into one of those career women who eventually got married by the time they were somebody quite different and aged about twenty-seven, and that in the intervening period boys were just not her scene.

'Forget it,' said Pete, though Ruth had still said nothing, for she could think of nothing to say. 'We'll walk this last bit. We've got plenty of time.'

'Pete,' said Ruth, evenly, 'do you often kiss girls?'

'Nope,' said Pete. 'Just thought I'd try it. Girls smell nicer than boys when they've gone for twenty-four hours without washing.'

'Thanks.'

'Well, you do, anyway. I don't know about other girls.'

Ruth turned round to look at him. His face was close behind hers, and beneath the smudges of dirt and the freckles he looked a shade thinner and paler than usual, and puffy under the eyes. She returned the kiss, politely, on the end of his nose.

'That's the only clean bit I can find,' she said. 'You look awfully tired.'

'Whose fault is that? You don't look too bright yourself.'

'I'm sorry. You didn't *need* to have come.'

'I'd have looked a bit silly if they'd found out what you were up to.'

'I'm glad you did come, anyway. Thanks a lot, Pete.'

'One thing, I'll be able to sleep all day. You won't.'

'I won't be able to do anything else, you mean, and nor will Tony. Uncle Sam will be rather surprised if he picks us up straight after breakfast and we both promptly go to sleep all the way to Newport.'

'You'll have to say Tony was too excited to sleep, and kept waking you up.'

'Poor old Tony.'

'Well, he did start all this, didn't he? I was quite surprised. I didn't think he had it in him. What made you realize he'd gone?'

Ruth filled in some of the gaps in yesterday's adventures. Tony had told Pete a certain amount when they had been riding together, but not Ruth's side of the story from the time Pete went up to Tygwyn and she met Gary at the post-office.

After she had told him about her encounter with Old Mossy on the hillside, Pete said, 'That reminds me, I discovered something surprising about Old Mossy yesterday. Did you know he was Tom's uncle?'

'*Tom's* uncle?'

'Yes. Uncle Sam told me. Apparently he's a brother of Tom's father.'

John Thomas was the biggest farmer in Llanwern, a member of the County Council, and a prominent figure in all the local affairs. Old Mossy seemed a very unlikely brother for him to have. But Ruth remembered him talking about John's wife, who gave him vegetables and knew how old he was, and he hoped was not going to see him put into a Home; and she remembered Gary remarking that Old Mossy was always up around Thomas's farm, and that his mother said there was no harm in him. But Gary had not sounded as though he knew Old Mossy was his uncle.

'But surely, if that were true, you'd have known? Tom and Gary would have known?'

'I said that, but Uncle Sam said with all the boys making such fun of Old Mossy, and him being something of a tramp, he thought they kept a bit quiet about the relationship, and maybe the younger boys didn't know. He thought Tom had probably tumbled to it by now, but not Gary.'

'How does Uncle Sam know?'

'He remembers him in school. He and Auntie Sybil were at school in Llanwern with Mr Thomas and Old Mossy, and Old Mossy was a bit of a joke even then. He was simple, you know – Uncle Sam used to share a desk with him, and he could never even learn to read and write. Your mum and Mr Thomas were younger, but John – Mr Thomas, you know – was always ahead of him in school work, right from the start.'

'What made Uncle Sam tell you all this?'

'It was after you rang off last night – you know, when the plans changed.'

'Yes. I wanted to call back after to find out if he'd discovered anything, but of course I couldn't.'

'Anyway, it was O.K. He wanted to know where you were, of course, because of telling you about Auntie Sybil being fine after the operation, and about Patsy. At first, when I told him you'd gone to fetch Tony, he said he'd wait, and that got me worried, so I said you might be ages, because Mossy had got some animals he wanted to show Tony, and you might have gone with them. I was afraid he might say you shouldn't go wandering off in the woods with Old Mossy, but he just laughed, and said something about Mossy never growing up. Uncle Sam said he remembered having a fight with him when they were boys, because he found Mossy setting loose some rabbits he had snared. Then he got to talk about them all being boys together at school and how Old Mossy was Mr Thomas's brother. Then he saw how late it was, and remembered he'd promised to go up to Grandad's to see about something in the garden with him, and he said if you and Tony didn't get back soon, to pop up on the bike and let him know. Of course, he didn't know you'd pinched my bike.'

'You don't suppose he came round after he got back?'

'I don't think he can have, because if he went into the house he'd have found my note, and gone chasing after you.'

When they got to the bridge, there was no sign of Tony, or the bike, and Pete was just beginning to say he must have been stupid and gone on into the village when Tony burst out on them with a 'Bo!' He had hidden the bike behind the parapet of the bridge.

'I've been here ages,' said Tony. 'What have you been doing all this time?'

'We won't go up the lane at all,' said Pete, ignoring this. There was a triangle of lanes from where they stood. The one to the left ran alongside the stream till it joined the main road at the bottom of the village and the other one kept straight on past Tygwyn and joined the same road above the village. The triangle was filled with the one big Tygwyn field, and Pete's back garden opened on to it. It was the field they always crossed to go to Tygwyn, and Betty lived in it. Already she was pressing eagerly against the gate.

'Tell you what,' said Pete. 'We can leave the saddle and bridle in the old barn for now, and I can take them back later on after you've gone. We might as well leave the bike there, too, because we'd be safer to keep round by the trees along the stream, and we won't be so noticeable without the bike.' The old barn was only fifty yards from where they stood, and close to the alders by the stream.

Behind the barn, they let Betty go. Tony hugged her, and thanked her, and promised to come and talk to her every day. She waited, polite and imperturbable, until he released her, and then moved off down to the stream, twitching the skin on her back where the saddle had been, nose close to the ground. She drank deeply, and then found a dry tussocky piece of ground to roll on with a flurry of legs in the air. Ruth watched her with an affection she had never thought to feel for a horse.

'Come on,' said Pete. 'Let's know the worst.'

A sudden sense of urgency swept over them, and they ran as fast as they could, crouching through the trees, and up close behind the hedge till they came to the gate into the garden.

For a moment Ruth paused here, remembering how she had stood at this same gate, less than three weeks ago, desolate and aloof. Soon she would be starting on a new life with her mother and Patsy and Tony, and perhaps sharing the routine of school bus and village activities with Pete and his friends. She watched Tony running up the path ahead of her, and remembered what Pete had said about learning a lot about his father when circumstances had thrown them unexpectedly together.

'Come on,' said Pete, and they hurried into the house after Tony, linked in a shared sense of anxious expectancy.

The house stood silent. They ran into the kitchen, and there, on the table, lay Pete's note, with UNCLE SAM written across it in large letters.

'We've made it!' said Ruth. Pete nodded, grinning.

'Hey!' said Tony, appearing with a basket of delectable-looking fresh mushrooms. 'What are these doing here?'

'Where did you find them?' asked Ruth.

'Here,' said Tony. 'Just inside the door.' The back door opened straight into the kitchen, but a second door led into a larder partitioned off from the main kitchen immediately on the left, making a small passageway where the mushrooms had been discovered.

'Uncle Sam must have brought them,' said Pete.

'Then he must have read your note,' said Ruth.

'That's funny. Where is he now, then?' They stood looking at each other, puzzled, until Pete said, 'It didn't *look* as though anyone had seen it. It was lying exactly as I left it.'

'You're not the only one who writes notes,' said Tony.

'No, you do,' said Ruth.

'And you,' said Pete.

'And Uncle Sam,' said Tony.

'Eh?' Ruth and Pete spoke at once.

Tony picked up a scrap of paper from among the mushrooms. On it was written in Uncle Sam's neat police hand:

Glad to see you've all gone to bed early. You ought to lock the back door. Grandpa sent these; he thought you might like them for breakfast.

'You bet we would,' said Pete. 'Anyone not like mushrooms?'

'No such luck,' said Ruth. 'Pete, do you mean he came right in here and never saw your note?'

'He never saw mine, either,' said Tony, and he turned over the scrap of paper on which Uncle Sam had written his message. On the back was the note Tony had left for them the morning before: 'I have gone for a visit and will not be back till evening. Please dont tell Uncle Sam or anyboddy becuase I am okay Tony.'

For a moment, they all three just stood there; then they laughed.

'You've only got an hour before Uncle Sam comes for you, and you've got a fair amount of washing to do,' said Pete. 'Let's get at those mushrooms.'